ENDLESS LOVE

Twenty years ago Gemma Sommerby and Jack Watson shared a summer romance, but after he left Cornwall she never heard from him again. And now, large as life and twice as handsome, he's back . . . Gemma can't afford to open her heart to him and risk being hurt again — and Jack is just as disconcerted to find she affects him as much as ever. Why did it really go wrong between them all those years ago? And could they still have a future together?

ANGELA BRITNELL

ENDLESS LOVE

Complete and Unabridged

LINFORD
Leicester

First published in Great Britain in 2015

First Linford Edition
published 2016

A catalogue record for this book is available
from the British Library.

ISBN 978–1–4448–2980–8

Published by
F. A. Thorpe (Publishing)
Anstey, Leicestershire

Set by Words & Graphics Ltd.
Anstey, Leicestershire
Printed and bound in Great Britain by
T. J. International Ltd., Padstow, Cornwall

This book is printed on acid-free paper

1

Gemma hid behind a rack of postcards and checked out the good-looking man now standing across the road and staring at her shop window. There was no doubt in her mind. Jack Watson was back. Judging by the flashy red sports car he was standing next to, he'd done well for himself since leaving town twenty years ago, exactly as he'd promised he would. Jack had made her a lot of promises too — but he'd kept none of them.

Her heart raced as he stepped down off the pavement and headed her way. She wondered if she could wave a magic wand and disappear into the ether. *Don't be stupid. You're a grown woman, not a teenager.* All they'd shared was a brief teenage romance one summer — no doubt long forgotten on his side. But Jack wasn't the kind of boy a girl ever forgot.

The tinkling doorbell forced Gemma to emerge from her hiding place, and as she did she plastered on a bright smile.

'I'm looking for . . . ' Jack pulled off a pair of designer sunglasses and Gemma struggled not to flinch as his intense green eyes swept down over her. A rush of heat coloured her neck and crept up to flood her cheeks. Idiotically, she wished she wasn't wearing her oldest pair of jeans and the yellow t-shirt she'd almost given to the charity shop before deciding it would do a little longer. 'Well, well, well. I don't believe it.' A touch of amusement pulled at the corners of his mouth. 'Gemma Sommerby. Still here. I'm surprised.'

She tilted her chin and faced his curious gaze straight on. 'I can't imagine why. This is my family's business, after all.' He didn't answer; only continued to study her as if he was a scientist and she was an interesting bug under a microscope. Objectively she noted the fact he'd grown into his unusual looks. Tall and gangly at seventeen, his green-as-glass eyes, shaggy black hair, and olive skin had always hinted at his mixed Italian/English heritage. Compared to the local Cornish boys she'd grown up with, Jack had been exotic, and he still was. Now everything about him looked expensive, from his immaculate haircut to the black leather jacket that she guessed cost more than she made in a year. The transatlantic edge to his deep, smooth voice was new as well, taking the edge off the posh accent her father always teased him about.

'You were bottom of the list of people I expected to come across,' he said.

Gemma shrugged, not about to get into a conversation about her life over the last twenty years. 'Did you come in here for a reason?'

'Yeah, I need directions to West Dean House.'

She waited for him to give her more details but he left it at that, making her feel awkward. Succinctly she rattled off directions, wondering why he wanted to know about the old Dean estate in the first place. The large, ramshackle house had fallen into disrepair when Walter Dean passed away several years ago and there'd been numerous rumours about what might happen to it. Gemma couldn't imagine what connection Jack might have to West Dean House, but her innate curiosity longed to find out.

* * *

Jack was relieved she was too polite to ask any more questions because he really didn't want to lie to her. *Again.* He wasn't at liberty to reveal his interest in the Dean estate, and his planned agenda was to get in and out of Cornwall as fast as possible.

'Does that all make sense?' she said.

He started as Gemma touched his arm. 'Sorry, did you say something?' Not paying attention was unusual for Jack. He was renowned for his quick intelligence and the fact no one ever had to tell him anything twice. Both traits he'd learned the hard way.

'I asked if my directions made sense.'

'Oh, yeah, thanks.' He ought to leave, but couldn't stop gazing at Gemma. Something about her bothered him, and not simply the way she'd turned into a very beautiful woman, although that too was disturbing. Her soft grey eyes were feathered with tiny lines at the corners and there was a tightness to her mouth hinting at strain and maybe even unhappiness. Jack pulled his attention back to the task in hand and stuck out his hand knowing he needed to get out of there, fast. 'I appreciate the help.'

With a definite hint of amusement she shook his hand, and Jack flushed with embarrassment. Treating her like an unknown shop assistant was juvenile, but she'd unconsciously sent him back to his unsure teenage self — a place Jack hadn't visited in a long time and where he had no desire to return.

'You're welcome. Good luck.'

'I might see you around.' He'd no idea why those words flew out of his mouth. This project would be challenge enough, and Gemma was a complication he didn't need.

'Maybe.' Why did it irk him that she didn't fall over herself? 'If you'll excuse me, I've got work to do.'

There were no customers and it was nearly closing time, but he held his tongue. For all he knew, she had a husband and four kids to go home to, although he'd taken note of her ringless left hand.

'Of course.' Jack turned and headed back out of the door before he could do something really stupid like ask her to join him for a drink later.

He hurried back over to his car, unlocking it with the remote on the way, and jumped right in. A man walking by gave the Porsche an envious glance as Jack started her up, so he gave the powerful engine an unnecessary rev before pulling out and driving off. Being early October, he'd only have about another hour of good daylight left to scope out the house and grounds. His boss expected a preliminary report by the middle of the week, so there was no time to waste.

He eased off the accelerator as he left the village in his rear-view mirror. He hadn't expected ever to return to Trewarne and didn't care for the unsettled feeling lurking in the pit of his stomach. But he'd been given no choice, and success here could mean achieving his goal to be a millionaire by the time he was forty. He'd done everything else he said he would.

You didn't go back for Gemma, he contradicted himself.

Pushing the unwelcome memory away, he concentrated on the narrow road and spotted a sign for West Dean House. He stopped in front of the rusting iron gates lashed together with a padlocked chain and got out of the car. After a couple of hard shakes the lock fell apart and he untangled the chain, tossing it to the ground. He pushed the gates open, shoving them over the tufts of grass growing up through the gravel.

Back in the car, he started down the drive, and within a few metres needed to switch on his lights when the overgrown trees and bushes lining the road sucked out the last of the daylight. He negotiated the frequent potholes and steered around fallen branches and mounds of wet leaves, beginning to wonder after about half a mile why there was no sign of any house or outbuildings. He carefully rounded another corner and slammed on his brakes. Through the mist rolling in from the nearby sea, West Dean House emerged to fill his vision, and instantly Jack knew this was exactly what his boss was looking for.

2

'Is that you, Gem?'

Gemma hung up her wet mac and kicked off her shoes before stepping into the cramped living room, forcing down a sigh. Judging by the dirty cups and piles of newspapers strewn over the coffee table, she suspected Harry hadn't made it any further than the kitchen all day. 'Who'd you think it was? Kate Moss come to take you out to a wild party?' she teased her brother, happy when a shy half-smile flitted across his serious features.

'Chance would be a fine thing, Gem.'

She swallowed hard and put on a bright smile in return. 'I'll get on with the tea. Will beans on toast do?' Today had drained her, and she didn't have the energy for anything more complicated before going out again later.

'My favourite.' For a second Gemma caught a glimpse of his old wicked sense of humour and she hurried off into the kitchen. Resting her hands on the counter for a moment, she took several long, steadying breaths.

Her brother was the answer to Jack's question of why she was still here. Three years older than her, he'd begged their parents for a motorbike, and they'd given him one for his twenty-first birthday. The combination of no helmet, Harry showing off for a new girlfriend, and a wet road changed his life. He'd been in hospital and a rehabilitation facility for months afterwards. Physically he'd largely recovered from his injuries, apart from a tendency to limp when he got tired and a lack of strength in his left arm. The memory problems it'd left him with were another story. He'd lost a large chunk of time completely, and others were intermittent, meaning some days were better than others. It'd left him unable to hold down a steady job, although he frequently picked up temporary work around the village from people who knew him.

'You okay, Gem?' Harry appeared in the kitchen, frowning at her. 'I'm sorry, you know.'

'What for?'

He pointed to his chest. 'Me. Everything.'

Gemma hurried over to wrap her arms around him, pulling him into a tight hug. 'Don't ever say that again. I love you, silly boy. We're okay together.' She eased back and smiled, a genuine one this time. 'Put the kettle on to boil. I'm gasping.'

Harry studied her, and she sensed he was about to say something else. But without another word he did what she asked, and they companionably got their meal ready together.

Sitting down at the table, they didn't talk much for a few minutes. Gemma considered telling Harry about seeing Jack, but if he couldn't remember it'd only frustrate him.

'Was the shop busy today?' Harry asked her.

If only. The small gift shop her parents started when she was a little girl was a struggle to keep going. It wouldn't have been her choice of a job, but with the loss of both their parents and Harry's challenges, she'd dropped out after her first year at university and pushed the idea of becoming a history teacher from her mind. Memories of laying on Porthpean beach in the hot sand with Jack as they idly talked about their plans for the future flooded back. He'd been determined to set the music world on its head with his spectacular voice; but seeing him today with his designer suit and fancy car, Gemma guessed his dreams had shifted too.

'Gem? What's up? We don't need you going into a daze when people speak to you as well.'

Harry's attempt to crack a joke startled her. Was that a good sign? He'd rarely made fun of himself since the accident, although before it his sharp, dry humour was legendary. 'You're right,' she said. 'Sorry. I was thinking.'

'I'll have to use that line myself.' Harry's quirky smile lifted her spirits, but she ordered herself not to get her hopes up. Tomorrow they could be back to square one again.

'You will indeed,' she went along with him, hating to dampen his good mood. 'There weren't many people in. About normal for early October.' She couldn't resist asking, 'Does the name Jack Watson mean anything to you?'

Harry frowned and pushed his baked beans around the plate. 'Jack?'

'Doesn't matter.' She picked up on the agitation in his voice, always a sure sign he was struggling to put things together and failing.

'If it wasn't important you wouldn't have asked me, Gem,' he murmured. 'It's almost there.' He tapped the side of his head and suddenly a big grin stretched across his face. 'Your boy-friend. Big bloke. Black hair. Green eyes. Talked funny.'

Gemma blushed and nodded. 'He came into the shop today.' Hurriedly she told him the rest of the story, leaving out the part about how disconcerted it'd made her. That was something for her to think about later, alone.

'Lucky man.'

It hadn't occurred to her Harry might be envious. She could've smacked herself for going on about Jack's smart appearance and flashy car. The two men were a similar age, but the difference in their lives couldn't have been clearer. 'Anyway, I don't suppose I'll see him again.' Changing the subject was best for both their sakes. She didn't need to mope over Jack Watson another minute. 'What's on the telly tonight?'

He gave her a long, hard look before answering. Hopefully by tomorrow he'd forget all about Jack — exactly the same as she intended.

★ ★ ★

Jack swept the powerful torch beam around what'd once been a grand entrance hall, brushing a spider web from his hair when he got too close to the perilously dangling chandelier. He didn't risk going upstairs, and probably wouldn't even in daylight until he'd got a structural engineer to check it out. If he could work his magic here in three short months, Thea Barrington would be one lucky woman when Paul gave her West Dean House as a wedding present. His reclusive boss's only request was that the house be remote, and Cornwall definitely fitted the bill, with bells on. Jack would score a huge bonus for tracking down this place; and if he could transform it into Thea's vision of an English stately home, he could retire if he chose to. *Retire? What would I do?* The desire to prove himself drove him continually, which was why twenty-hour work days were routine and he considered sleep nothing more than a necessary evil.

He cautiously opened a set of double

doors and stared in awe at the huge ballroom in front of him. Pointing his torch at the walls, Jack made out faded gold scrollwork and dirty outlines where paintings must've hung. It wasn't hard to imagine the glamorous Thea hosting parties and bringing the house back to life. He hummed a Strauss waltz and then eased into a long-forgotten Verdi aria from *Rigoletto*. His rusty voice soared in the empty room, and a flicker of joy he hadn't felt in years stirred deep in his soul.

His father's mockery echoed through the musty air and he fell silent. *Forget this music nonsense. You're not good enough. Live with it.*

Jack kicked at a moth-eaten rug and stalked out of the room, slamming the doors shut behind him. He'd go back to the Green Dragon pub in the village and see if they had a room available. They'd need to have a decent Wi-Fi connection so he could keep up with his boss back in Nashville. Paul would expect constant updates on how things were going. He rubbed at the nagging headache pulsing at his temples. The combination of using the company's private jet and self-discipline usually meant jet lag wasn't an issue for him, but that wasn't working today.

Be honest. Seeing Gemma again was the cause. She brought back too many memories of a time when he'd been carefree and full of optimism, before everything fell apart. The urge to put his arms around Gemma earlier and beg her forgiveness had stretched his control to breaking point.

Back outside in the car, Jack rested his hands on the steering wheel and waited until the dangerous mood passed before turning on the engine and slowly pulling away from the house. One way or another, he was going to earn every penny he made on this job.

3

Gemma checked her watch and sighed. 'Time for me to go to work, Harry.'

'I wish you didn't have to,' he moaned.

You and me both. The only way she could juggle the never-ending bills was to pick up any extra jobs she could fit in. She did a couple of part-time cleaning jobs at houses in the village and turned into a barmaid when Bert needed extra help at the Green Dragon. Tonight she was going in at eight until closing time because Maisy was sick.

'You can watch the new DVD I brought home. Tell me what it's like when I get back.' She heaved herself up from the sofa and stretched out her tired arms. Glancing down, she decided she'd have to change. Bert wouldn't complain, but she owed him better than the dreary clothes she'd worked in all day.

'Maybe I'll pop in for a drink later,' Harry said. They both knew he wouldn't, because he found social situations awkward these days.

'You do that,' she played along. 'I must go and change.'

Gemma disappeared up to her bedroom and grabbed the only clean blouse hanging in her wardrobe, a plain cream one that'd seen better days. She teamed it with a narrow black skirt and black wedge shoes before undoing the tight ponytail she'd had her hair up in all day and tugged a brush through her shoulder-length auburn curls, noticing a few strands of grey that hadn't been there last time she checked. *You're nearly forty. What do you expect?*

With a quick slick of pink lip gloss she was done, and hurried back downstairs. 'Bye, Harry,' she said. 'I put my mobile number by the phone if you need me.'

He barely looked up from the action

film he was already engrossed in, so Gemma threw on her mac and ran out of the door. Luckily it was only a five-minute walk. The earlier rain had stopped, so she forced herself to slow down. She sucked in a few breaths of the fresh, salty air and stopped a minute to check out the clear night sky before keeping going. The tourist season was pretty much over, but because it was a Friday night there'd be a few more people in the pub. Thankfully, most of the youngsters hung out at the noisier Duke of Wellington closer to the harbour — dealing with mouthy teenagers wasn't her favourite way to spend an evening.

Gemma breezed into the pub and shouted hello to Bert, greeted a few of the locals, and went to hang up her coat. Just as she was about to start picking up glasses, someone tapped her arm.

'Long time, no see.' Jack's deep, smooth voice next to her shoulder made her jump. The transatlantic accent she'd picked up on earlier was more pronounced now and made her even more curious about where he'd spent the last twenty years. 'Are you meeting someone?'

An irrational urge to produce a boyfriend out of thin air swept through her, but honesty won out and she shook her head. It'd be pretty obvious soon, so what was the point? 'I'm about to start work.'

'Another job? You're a busy lady.'

She bit her tongue, hating the patronising edge to his words. What would he know about struggling to make ends meet with his expensive car and designer clothes? The boy she remembered would've understood. Back then, Jack had been sent from London to stay for the summer with his elderly aunt and was always grateful when Gemma's mother invited him for a meal.

'Sorry.' He touched her forearm, and the warmth of his fingers pressed through her thin blouse. 'I didn't mean to be rude.' Jack's sharp-eyed gaze pierced through her and Gemma struggled to breathe. Years ago every time he looked at her that way she'd melted. 'Forgive me?'

'There's nothing to forgive.' She took a step away from Jack and his arm dropped back down to his side. 'I need to start work.'

Jack nodded. 'I'm staying here for a few days. I've just ordered some food.'

'Oh, right. Enjoy yourself.' Before he could detain her any longer, Gemma hurried off towards the back of the room, as far away from Jack Watson as she could get.

* * *

Nice one, Jack. He didn't have a clue why his usual good manners deserted him around Gemma, but they did, and he became gauche and inconsiderate. Anyone would think he was a naive teenaged boy instead of a wealthy thirty-seven-year old businessman. *Yeah, but she still sees the boy, albeit with a glossy surface that means nothing to her.* He'd eat his dinner quickly when it arrived and clear off upstairs to his room. Earlier he'd successfully caught up with his accumulated emails and made a few phone calls. Paul Von Doorsten wasn't a man to sound excited about anything — he was too much of a pragmatist for that — but there'd been a hint of pleasure as he listened to what Jack had achieved so far.

'Sausage, mash and beans.'

He glanced up to meet Gemma's amused smile as she held out a loaded plate.

'Some things never change,' she joked, and he couldn't resist smiling right back. Years ago it'd been his favourite meal. He'd loved her mother's sausages — good meaty ones from the local butcher instead of the cheap ones that were all his aunt could afford.

'Does your mother still cook them every Wednesday?' he asked her.

A shadow crossed her face. 'She

passed away a long time ago. My father too.'

'I'm sorry.' Jack instinctively reached out to cover her hand with his own and caressed her soft, warm skin in an attempt to give some measure of comfort. 'Did Harry ever make anything of his art? I remember how talented he was. Or does he work with you in the shop?'

'Harry lives with me but he doesn't work in the shop.' Gemma's halting explanation obviously caused her distress and he longed to tell her to stop; that it was none of his business. They both had their secrets. 'It's complicated. Let's leave it there, okay?' Her voice wobbled and she pulled her hand away. 'Enjoy your meal.' She rushed off as though a pack of hounds was chasing her. Jack almost went after her, but made himself pick up his knife and fork and start to eat. He'd upset her enough today already.

He shovelled the food down, barely tasting anything, and pushed the empty plate away. If he tried to sleep this early it'd be a miserable failure, but a short walk down to the harbour might help him unwind. Jack left a generous tip on the table, hoping Gemma wouldn't misinterpret that too. He wended his way through the crowded bar and pushed open the door to step outside. A blast of brisk, salty air hit him in the face and Jack shivered in his thin shirt. He considered going back to his room for a sweater but abandoned the idea and kept walking.

As he wandered down around the corner from the pub, he stopped instinctively outside the small café where he and Gemma sometimes hung out. Jack couldn't believe it was still in business. They used to laugh because it'd been called Le Grand Café, a wildly inappropriate name considering the pedestrian nature of its offerings. He could count on one hand the number of times they'd had enough money for a cup of tea there and only one occasion when they'd indulged in cake as well:

Gemma's seventeenth birthday. Her beautiful face had shone with happiness as she relished every bite of the chocolate and orange cake it'd taken her at least ten minutes to decide on. That'd been Jack's only gift to her, and she couldn't have been happier.

He mentally compared her to his latest ex-girlfriend. Jack had flown Briony to New York in the company's private jet to see a top-rated Broadway show, followed by dinner at a fancy restaurant, and then he'd produced an expensive Tiffany necklace for her birthday present. But all she'd done was complain about everything and then dump him the next day because she'd apparently expected a proposal, something he'd given her no reason to believe was imminent. Gemma, on the other hand, had enjoyed every moment they spent together and helped to make everything they did special, no matter how mundane. But he'd let her down, and by her wariness today he knew it hadn't been forgotten.

Why should she? he mused. *You've harboured some resentments for a very long time yourself. They're what drive you to get up every day and push harder and harder to prove your father wrong.*

Jack shoved his hands in his pockets and put his head down and kept walking. A gang of noisy teenaged boys jostled each other and yelled obscenities outside the Duke of Wellington pub. He smiled to himself as his Aunty Marion's warnings from that long-ago summer echoed in his head: 'I know you're a big lad and can take care of yourself, but don't do anything daft or your father will skin us both. Stay away from the Welly pub. All the louts go there, and they do say there's drugs and stuff going on.'

She'd been a kind woman, lumbered with a nephew she barely knew who resented being sent to Cornwall for the summer away from all his mates. It'd helped that she had no more love for his father than Jack did. They'd rubbed along well enough, and by the end of August he'd been sorry to leave. He'd been even sorrier just after Christmas when Marion didn't survive a bout of pneumonia. When Jack told his father he wanted to go to her funeral, he was coldly informed it'd taken place the week before. Flowers had been sent from the family and that was considered sufficient.

No wonder he'd closed down his heart. He hadn't been worthy of Gemma's love then, or anyone else's since.

Jack's phone vibrated in his pocket and he yanked it out, checking the number before he answered. 'Watson here.'

Paul Von Doorsten immediately launched into a whole new round of instructions, and Jack forced himself to concentrate on what his boss was saying. With a huge sense of relief, he pushed away the nonsense in his head and switched back into work mode. He'd carved out his own life and was exactly where he wanted to be. The rest was pointless, and he refused to waste another moment on it.

'Sure, Paul, everything's on track. I'm your man and I won't let you down.'

He could keep that sort of promise. He hadn't fought this hard to leave his old life behind to fail at anything.

4

The shop door bounced back and hit the wall, sending the chimes into a frantic jangle. Gemma glanced up from pricing a new range of singing pixie charms to see her best friend standing there with a distinctly annoyed look on her face. April's wet blond curls hung around her shoulders like strands of overcooked spaghetti, and if she hadn't been glaring so fiercely Gemma would've laughed. Plainly the idea of wearing a mac or carrying an umbrella hadn't occurred to her.

'Some sort of best mate you are. You don't tell me anything,' April protested shrilly.

'What on earth are you talking about?'

She pointed her finger in Gemma's face. 'What do you think? Jack Watson. You didn't think the fact that the man you've mooned over for decades came back yesterday was news?'

Gemma tried to protest but it was hopeless. There was no point pretending she hadn't mentioned Jack a few times over the years. *Make that a few thousand times.* Most of the girls she'd gone to school with had either left the village, or stayed and were married with kids by now. She and April were the lone hangouts who'd done neither. April's family owned a shop too, but unlike Gemma's gift shop, the Broad family's Cornish fudge shop was successful.

'Bert Hendra came in this morning bragging about a wealthy Yank he had staying,' April said. 'When he mentioned the name and described him, I knew. I don't know why he called him a Yank, though.' She fixed Gemma with another hard stare. 'Have you seen him?'

A heavy sigh escaped before Gemma could stop it. 'Yes. Twice.' She rushed to tell the whole story before she could be berated any further. 'I did catch a slight American accent, so I'd guess he's been living over there.'

'How did he look?'

Gorgeous. Out of my league. Exactly the same when I looked in his eyes. 'Oh, you know,' she said aloud.

'No, I don't. That's why I'm asking.' A sly smile crept over April's face. 'You still fancy him, don't you?'

Gemma blushed. 'He's a good-looking man. I may not get out much, but I'm still a woman and have normal . . . feelings.' She opened another box of pixie charms and started to take them out of the plastic bags. 'Nothing's going to happen, April. I'm not Cinderella and Jack isn't going to be my Prince Charming, so stop the fantasy right now.' She glanced up. 'For someone whose social life is as pathetic as mine, you're an incurable romantic.' A flare of pain darkened April's bright blue eyes and she immediately regretted speaking.

'That's the last thing I am, Gemma.'

April's quiet, broken words echoed in the empty shop. As teenagers, Harry and April had been madly in love. The two girls would joke about becoming real-life sisters one day and spent endless hours planning the extravagant double wedding they'd have. When her brother's head was turned by a glamorous girl on holiday from London, leading to his accident, it'd shattered more than his own dreams.

Gemma wrapped her arms around her friend in a warm hug. 'Sorry. That was thoughtless.'

'It's been a long time. I should be over it.'

'Some of us aren't wired that way, are we?' Gemma sighed. 'I hadn't seen Jack for twenty years, but when he walked back into this shop it might as well have been yesterday. And you've been around Harry all this time. I can't imagine how painful it's been.'

April pulled away, her eyes brimming over with tears. 'With all the memories that have come back to him over the years, he's never remembered . . . us, and how we were together. I know we were young, but it still meant something.' She rubbed at her wet hair as if she'd suddenly realised it was a mess. 'For his sake it may be just as well, but . . . '

'It breaks your heart.' Gemma's quiet statement fell between them into the silence. 'I wish things could be different.'

'You know what they say — if wishes were horses, beggars would ride.' The rare harsh tone of April's voice took Gemma by surprise. Her friend was always the softer, kinder one of the two of them, but plainly Gemma had hit a nerve. 'I'd better go,' April added, 'or Mum will wonder where I am.' Mrs. Broad kept a close eye on her only child and wasn't disappointed that April was still single and living at home.

'Do you fancy going for a drink later?' Gemma offered, although it was one of her rare nights off and she had a million things to catch up on. 'Anywhere but the Green Dragon.' Staying well away from Jack Watson's orbit was number one on her to-do list right now.

April shook her head. 'Wish I could, but it's Women's Institute night and I've got to take Mum.'

'Another time.' They understood and accepted each other's limitations; it was the main reason they'd remained such good friends and would do anything for each other.

April's brave smile returned. 'Bye. Behave yourself,' she joked on her way out, and Gemma tried to smile back.

Left to her singing pixie charms, it was set to be a long afternoon.

★ ★ ★

Practical jeans, a warm flannel shirt, and sturdy work boots made for an easier time poking around West Dean House. So did daylight. Money talked, and Jack already held a preliminary report from the structural engineer in his hands. It wasn't as depressing as he'd expected. Although Walter Dean had sorely neglected the fabric of the house, living in two small downstairs rooms and locking up the rest of the house, the shell was in remarkably good shape. The roof only needed minor repairs, and the staircase and wood floors were basically sound. It'd need complete rewiring, but Jack had a couple of electricians lined up to come to the house and give him estimates that afternoon. Before he left Nashville he'd already been in touch with several Cornish companies who specialised in period redecoration in older homes and instructed them to start on preliminary research, ready to go to work if he gave the word.

Jack's spirits rose. If he could pull this off in the tight time frame he had, his reputation would be made. He was a fixer. Give him a problem and he'd solve it. His genius was in delegation — finding the right people to do the necessary work at the best quality and price. Von Doorsten Industries was a huge company and Paul's interests were varied, meaning Jack's job was never the same from day to day. His boss used him for projects that didn't fit into the normal run of things, and West Dean House definitely fell under that heading. It'd struck him as amusing when his stoic, no-nonsense boss fell for Thea, Hollywood's top box-office star, but recent differences in the man unsettled him. Paul's focus wasn't as sharp, and he was more inclined to blow off work early to go home to his fiancée. One day Jack had been foolish enough to question him and had got his head bitten off.

'There's more to life than work, Jack,' Paul had told him. 'You could do with a good woman to humanise you, too.' He even gave Jack a patronising smile, as though he felt sorry for him. No one needed to be sorry for Jack Watson. Not anymore. He'd be careful not to cross that line again with Paul. They weren't friends. He was an employee and must remember the fact.

His phone buzzed and he answered right away. As a man's gruff voice spoke his name, Jack's world plunged into a rapid tailspin.

* * *

'April popped into the shop today,' Gemma said casually as she chopped onions and tossed them into a hot frying pan. Harry was sitting at the kitchen table peeling potatoes and didn't look up. 'I thought I might ask her to have supper with us one night.'

'If you want.'

'Would *you* like her to come?' Gemma wasn't sure why she was persisting, but something about her friend's sadness today had got to her.

Harry laid down the peeler. His deep-set eyes were a darker shade of grey than her own, and when he was excited or worried they turned almost black. Right now they resembled lumps of coal. 'Why wouldn't I? April's my friend. I like her. A lot.'

Gemma knew that if she carried on, Harry might get upset, and she'd be the one dealing with the aftermath. 'Of course you do,' she said mildly. 'I thought it'd be nice for us to have some company.' She turned back to her cooking. Stirring the onions around, she threw in a handful of mushrooms and a sliced green pepper. 'Are the potatoes ready? I need to get them in here, Harry.'

'I'll bring them.' He pushed his chair back and got up, then carried the chopping board over to her and tipped the diced potatoes into the pan. 'April's very pretty. She's got nice, kind eyes.'

Gemma's heart thumped and she tried to concentrate on her cooking as though they weren't having an important conversation. Harry never did well if he thought he was being analysed and picked apart.

'I wish . . . ' he began.

'What do you wish?' She glanced over her shoulder, taken aback by the pain etched into his face.

'I wish you'd hurry up and get our tea ready. I'm starving.' The firm, good-humoured statement was his way of ending of the conversation.

'Won't be long. The sausages are cooked.' Gemma's heart clenched. Why had it surprised her when Jack made a remark about her mother's sausages? His aunt had tried her best but hadn't had much money, and Jack was a growing boy who was always hungry. When her own mother guessed, she'd taken him under her wing. It hadn't made any difference to her if she was cooking for four or five and there was always plenty of food to go around. She'd liked the polite young man who treated her daughter well, and enjoyed his quick wit and good manners. None of them understood why Jack didn't answer any of Gemma's letters and never came back to Cornwall. Her mother held Gemma in her arms and rocked her to sleep while she cried her heart out over him, unable to come up with any reason for his abandonment.

'You're burning that.' Harry's sharp voice broke through Gemma's reverie and she jerked the pan off the heat, then stared at the charred mess as tears pricked at her eyes.

'Hey, it's all right, I like it well done. I've already shared the sausages out on the plates.' Harry's efforts to make her feel better touched her, because for a long time he'd lost the empathetic side of his personality. It'd crept back over the last few years and she was thankful.

She dished up the vegetables and carried the plates over to the table. 'There you go.'

'Thanks, Gem.'

They ate in silence, both wrapped in their own thoughts. Gemma wished hers didn't keep leading back to a man with beguiling green eyes and the key to her heart. Her life was challenging enough without Jack Watson complicating everything. Again.

5

'Are you there, son?'

'Yes, sir,' Jack replied, on automatic pilot. 'What do you want?'

'Your manners haven't improved.'

Instant condemnation. Why should he be surprised? Jack slumped down to sit on the bottom stair, afraid his legs wouldn't hold him up otherwise. He hadn't spoken to his father in so long, it shocked him to hear the usual harsh tones marred by an unmistakeable tremble. 'Are you well, sir?'

'Fine. Why wouldn't I be?'

I don't know. You tell me. You've rung for something and it's not simply to pass the time of day. 'It was merely a polite question, sir,' he said aloud.

'It's your mother.'

Jack's stomach churned as he caught his father's sharp intake of breath.

'She's not well and wants to see you.'

He tried to imagine what it'd cost his father to pick up the phone after their last bitter quarrel but failed. His mother must have a stronger hold on Philip than Jack had ever realised.

'I know you don't want to see me, and the feeling's mutual, but you'll do this for her.' There was no hint of pleading or softness, but Jack sensed the pain underneath his father's brusque statement. He hated the idea of having any sympathy for the man who'd treated his only son harsher than any of the soldiers under his command. 'We're still in Plymouth so there's no excuse. It's not far.'

'How did you know I was working nearby?'

Philip Watson's harsh laughter resonated down the line. 'Did you really think I haven't been keeping track of you and what you were doing?'

Jack hadn't given it much thought, because every time his parents entered his mind he deliberately pushed them back out again.

'You're doing well for yourself.' The grudging compliment stunned Jack. 'I suppose you're wasting it all on expensive cars and flashy clothes. You were always too fond of that sort of thing.' With a few well-chosen words he'd torn Jack back down to the place where he always kept his son. Jack needed to take several long, slow breaths to stop himself saying something he'd regret later. There'd been too much of that already and he refused to sink to that level again.

'When do you want me to come?' From experience he didn't bother mentioning when would be most convenient for himself, because that wouldn't be an issue as far as his father was concerned. When he told people to jump they jumped. All they asked was how high.

'Come to tea on Sunday. Four o'clock.'

The phone clicked and Jack realised his father had hung up. *See you Sunday*. He'd never understood why his beautiful Italian mother with her sparkling good looks and bright personality had married Philip Watson. Objectively his father had probably been a handsome young man, intelligent and hard-working, but even so they were an unlikely pair. It'd just about killed Jack to stop all contact with his mother, but it was the only way to save himself. He'd known his father would try to prevent her getting in touch, so had tried to make it easier on her by being the one to sever the connection.

He shoved his hand up through his hair in exasperation and realised it could do with a quick trim. He decided to take a break and get a bite of lunch in Trewarne before scouting around for a barber. The first electrician wasn't coming until two, so he should have plenty of time. He pulled himself back up to standing and hurried outside after making sure to lock up securely. First thing this morning he'd installed new deadbolts on all the outside doors.

There were still a couple of broken windows and places it was possible to get in, but Jack hoped it might deter the teenagers who'd been taking advantage of the empty house, judging by some of the litter he'd found. Once the restoration started, he'd employ a security company to keep an eye on the place. If it wasn't too late after his lunch and haircut, he'd go back to his room and upload the photos he'd taken that morning so Paul could see the full extent of what they were up against.

Humming the song he couldn't get out of his head after yesterday, Jack hopped into the Porsche and drove off slowly down the potholed drive back out to the main road. If he was going to be here a few months — and it looked increasingly likely — he'd need a more practical car and somewhere quieter to stay. He'd get the job done and deal with his parents, then head back to Nashville with his mission accomplished. Any idiotic notion he'd harboured about reconnecting with

46

Gemma needed to vanish. She was part of his past, which was precisely where he was going to keep her.

* * *

'We can't keep meeting like this.' Jack's teasing drawl made Gemma blush as he grasped hold of her elbow to stop her tripping right over him in the street. He'd stepped out of the barber's and she'd been daydreaming, idly wandering back to her shop after nipping out to post a few letters while things were quiet. 'You okay?'

'Of course.' She jerked away and brushed down her skirt, although it wasn't dirty or creased, needing something to do with her hands. 'Thank you.'

Before she could walk away he touched her again, resting a broad hand on her shoulder this time so she couldn't move. 'How about meeting me for a drink tonight so we can sort this out?'

Gemma struggled to keep her voice steady. 'I can't imagine what you're talking about. What can we possibly have to sort out?'

'You. Me. The past. I'm going to be around here for a while, and we can't keep tiptoeing around each other this way.'

Why not? She'd never been a great one for confrontation, and avoiding the subject of their brief romance and its aftermath would suit her perfectly.

The crinkly lines fanning out from the corners of his eyes told her he'd read her mind, exactly the way he used to, and found her reticence amusing. This new version of Jack was very different from the shy, thoughtful young man who'd won her heart. He'd turned into an efficient, decisive man who spoke his mind and wasted little time with pleasantries. *What a pity he still has the same killer smile.*

'I'm busy,' she said.

'Fine. Tell me when you're not and I'll be there.'

In my dreams? It's the only place you and I are going to meet anytime soon. I'm not totally stupid. 'There's nothing to sort.' Jack raised one straight, dark brow in obvious disbelief, but she ignored him. 'We had a teenage thing. We're grown-ups now. It's in the past. You do your job — whatever it is — and I'll do mine. I'm sure we're civilised enough to be polite when we meet.'

Jack's eyes gleamed, and as he stepped closer she caught a hint of his aftershave. The heady, expensive scent matched the rest of him. He might be wearing jeans and a checked shirt today, but Gemma recognised quality clothes when she saw them.

'I'll let you in on a secret,' he whispered, his warm breath caressing her skin as his lips almost brushed her cheek. 'If all goes well, I'll be working at West Dean House until the New Year.' He wagged his finger. 'Don't tell anyone. It's not official yet.'

She was bursting with curiosity but refused to indulge him. He'd simply told her in order to get her talking again, and she wouldn't fall for the obvious ploy. He must think she'd been born yesterday. 'I see no reason I'd be talking about *you* to *anyone*.' He didn't need to know she'd be on the phone to April the minute she got back to the shop. 'I hope it goes well. Now I really must go.'

Jack's gaze hardened, turning his eyes the colour of a frigid December sea. He moved his hand and stepped away. 'Fair enough.' Without another word he strode off, his long legs quickly taking him to the end of the street and around the corner out of her sight.

Gemma trembled from head to toe, resenting the strong effect he still had on her after all these years. 'Ouch.' She glanced at her hands and realised she'd dug her fingers in so hard she'd left sharp indentations in her palms. Why couldn't he have stayed away for another twenty years? Maybe by then she'd have got over loving Jack Watson.

★　★　★

Jack's blood boiled and he carried on walking, marching past the Green Dragon and all the way along the cliff path until he reached the old Huer's Hut. Rough white-capped waves crashed onto the beach below, matching the anger surging through his body. He shouldn't have come to this particular spot; it was the last place he and Gemma had met before he'd left. She'd explained to him that the small circular building was where the fisherman would stand to watch for shoals of pilchards so they knew when to send the boats out. That was all gone now, and the few boats left made their living taking tourists on pleasure trips mixed in with a little mackerel fishing.

He'd wrapped his arms around her, stroking her glorious auburn hair, and promised to return at Christmas. She'd smelt of love and the sea, her lips soft and warm when they kissed. The one question he'd ached to ask her today was why she'd never replied to any of his letters, but maybe he wouldn't have wanted to hear the answer. Once he'd gone, she'd obviously forgotten him. He only wished he'd been able to do the same; but the memories of her, and of them together, never left him. He'd gone out with many other women, but they'd never been Gemma. Now she'd made it clear she wanted nothing to do with him, and Jack was a pragmatic man. He'd draw a line under Gemma Sommerby's name and move on.

I'm sure we're civilised enough to be polite when we meet. He could do civilised. It'd been drummed into him since birth, so maybe his father's hard, unemotional child-rearing methods had benefits Jack hadn't noticed before. They'd made him strong enough not to need anyone else, and that was the best way to live.

Jack went back to work, because work never let him down.

6

'He asked me to meet him for a drink to 'sort things out'. Who does he think he is?' Gemma shrieked down the phone.

'I assume you told him where to go?' April ventured.

Gemma launched into the whole story, missing out the part about her trembling knees, Jack's delicious after-shave, and the almost irresistible urge she'd had to run her fingers through his smooth, freshly cut hair. 'I've still no idea what he's planning to do at West Dean House or how long 'a while' constitutes in Jack's language. He'd better not stay at the Green Dragon is all I know,' she complained.

'I'm sure he got the hint,' April tried to placate her, but Gemma rambled on. Luckily her friend was patient and made appropriate, soothing noises at regular intervals until Gemma finally ran out of steam.

'Sorry,' Gemma said sheepishly.

'No probs. You've listened to me moan enough times. It's what we do.'

Gemma needed to see her friend in person. 'Would you like to come over and have your tea with us tonight?' Even over the phone, she sensed April's hesitation. 'Harry said yesterday he hadn't seen you for ages.' That was close enough to being true.

'Why don't I believe you?'

Gemma gave up. 'Okay. It's me who wants to see you,' she hurried on. 'Not that Harry won't be pleased too. We never get a minute to gossip these days, and you always hear more news in the fudge shop — probably because you actually have customers.' If she had to make her friend feel sorry for her to get what she wanted, she'd happily humiliate herself. 'I'm making lasagne.' That was a really low blow. The Italian dish was April's favourite, and her parents refused to eat what they called 'foreign muck'.

April sighed. 'You win.'

'Good. Come at half-past six. I'll even have wine.'

'In that case I'll bring something for pudding. It'll be a treat for me too, because Mother's been driving me mad this week. I nearly brained her with the heaviest box of fudge today. She was only saved by nosey old Mrs. Hawkins coming in to tell us about Janey Wilkinson's latest exploits.'

'What's she done?'

'You'll have to wait until tonight to find out.' April's smug reply tickled Gemma's funny bone.

'I hate you.' She laughed, and it felt good to let loose. 'See you later.' Still laughing, she hung up the phone, amazed by how much better she felt. Jack Watson could take a running jump as far as she was concerned. She considering ringing Harry but changed her mind. In another hour she'd close up and be home, so if he hadn't taken the mince out of the freezer she'd still have time if she hurried up. If she told him April was coming, Gemma couldn't be sure how he'd react, so for now she'd simply look forward to the evening.

She kept busy with rearranging shelves and selling the grand total of one birthday card before finally turning over the 'closed' sign and locking the door. The she threw on her coat, grabbed her handbag, and hurried along the road. She popped into the corner shop for a bottle of wine and chanced their so-called 'Vintage of the Week'. Gemma suspected the cheap Italian red on a buy 'one get one free' deal might resemble aircraft fuel, but decided to live dangerously.

'Harry, I'm back,' she called out as she flung open the door. Her stomach always tightened until he replied, but tonight the delicious, heavy smell of garlic and tomatoes filled the air and Gemma's spirits lifted.

'In the kitchen.'

She went straight in without stopping

to take off her coat. Harry stood in front of the cooker, frowning and stirring the contents of a large saucepan. 'I remembered you wanted the meat sauce made, because I wrote it down and set a timer,' he said.

Gemma's eyes prickled. 'That's great.' She smiled. 'I hope you don't mind, but I asked April over. She loves lasagne and her mother won't let her make it at home. Says it's nasty stuff.'

'Mrs. Broad's an odd woman. I don't like her. She's not kind to April and she speaks to me as if I'm an idiot.' Harry didn't have much of a filter these days and his brutally honest comments sometimes took Gemma's breath away. He glanced back over his shoulder, his eyes dark with strain. 'I know I have some problems, but I'm not stupid.'

Gemma hurried over to hug him, slipping her hand around his waist and resting her head on his warm blue jumper. 'No, you're definitely not stupid, and she's a cruel woman.'

'We'll make sure April has a happy

evening. It hurts me when she's sad.'

Oh Harry, you're breaking my heart. Was she fooling herself to think there was any sort of chance for the two people she cared for so much? Yes, she probably was. But a life without hope wasn't much of a life at all, in her opinion.

★ ★ ★

A full week: that was how long it would take the electrician he'd hired to rewire West Dean House with his whole crew. The plumber was lined up, as soon as the electrical work was finished, to do some basic work before the real renovation started. Jack had put out feelers to a couple of local roofers, and making that decision was tomorrow's main task. After his run-in with Gemma, he'd gone to the nearest hardware store and bought a load of plywood. Boarding up the broken windows until they could be properly fixed worked off his excess energy and

58

made the house more secure.

Paul would've told him to pay someone else to do the donkey work, but the physical challenge suited Jack. He hated the idea of becoming a soft office type and frequently pitched in on different projects. As soon as there was a functioning bathroom, he'd decided to move out of the Green Dragon and camp here. It made sense on several different levels. The contractors would work harder if they didn't know when Jack was going to appear and check on them; plus he'd have his independence, something he valued more than money in the bank.

Jack didn't know a thing about paint colours and interior decoration but would outsource that side of the job. He had already sent details of several businesses available to take on the task to Paul for his consideration. They'd discuss it soon and narrow it down to two or three for Jack to interview. Once he'd made his recommendations it would be Paul's decision. Personally he thought Thea should be involved, but Paul insisted he knew her taste and wanted the house to be a complete surprise. Jack was afraid his boss would be the one getting a surprise, and not necessarily a pleasant one.

Landscaping the extensive grounds would be a huge task, but he'd put his foot down there. Three months was a crazy short time to get the inside sorted, and he'd told Paul the gardens would have to wait. He'd get someone to clear the driveway and put down fresh gravel, but that was as far as he would go. Paul knew that when Jack said something was impossible, he meant it.

The light was starting to fade, but Jack couldn't resist going back into the ballroom. He hoped Thea wouldn't bring her noisy Hollywood friends here. West Dean House was meant to be a gathering place for the local gentry — an antiquated notion these days; but Jack wanted to see Thea and Paul explore their own version. If they got to know some of the talented local artists and musicians, his reserved boss might find that socialising didn't have to be painful. Paul would never have met Thea in the first place, but his sister knew her and got the two of them together at a quiet dinner party.

Jack was drawn towards the old grand piano, long neglected and no doubt woefully out of tune. He dusted off the worst of the grime with his shirt sleeve and sat down on the rickety stool. Tentatively he tried out some scales and discovered several sticking notes. It sounded dreadful, but he started to pick out the basics of a Mozart piece from *Don Giovanni* that he remembered performing decades ago. His voice was as off as the piano, but he immersed himself in the music and lost himself in the joy of the glorious melody.

'Bravo.'

He jerked around with his face red as fire. A stunningly beautiful young woman stood in the doorway, clapping and laughing. She strode toward him, and all he noticed was her seemingly endless jean-clad legs, flashing sapphire eyes and shining blond hair.

'Hannah Petersen.' She stuck out her hand and he took it, surprised by her firm grip. 'Unique Restorations Company.'

'Oh.'

'I've been visiting a friend nearby and couldn't resist the chance to see around the house.'

Jack scrambled to get his brain back in gear. She was with one of the companies he'd recommended to Paul as possible contractors for the interior decoration. 'I did inform you we'd be in touch if we wanted you to submit a more detailed plan, and you'd get the opportunity to visit the house at that point,' he said. 'We're not there yet.'

Her mocking smile knocked him off kilter. 'I prefer to be ahead of things, Mr. — ?'

'Watson. Jack Watson.' He finally remembered his manners and stood up.

'Do excuse me. I wasn't expecting . . . '
His face heated again as he brushed globs of dirt from his jeans.

'Obviously,' she teased. 'I should apologise for dropping in on you, but I'm not going to.'

Why doesn't that surprise me? 'I appreciate your desire to be prepared. I work the same way.' He glanced down at himself, then back up at her, giving in to a smile. 'Usually.'

'You can make it up to me by giving me a quick tour and then taking me out to dinner,' Hannah declared with an impish grin.

'Of course.' He kept his voice crisp and businesslike. Perhaps he was being vain to think he'd picked up an interest on her part that didn't exist, and he preferred to be cautious.

Jack's hesitation lasted until they started the tour, but then Hannah's enthusiasm for the house excited him. She painted pictures with words, describing how she saw West Dean House developing and luring him into expressing his own visions for the place. He found himself describing how Paul saw the house through Thea's eyes before realising he was being unprofessional. 'Um, I shouldn't be sharing all this with you. It might give you an unfair advantage over the other businesses we're looking at.'

Her eyes softened. 'I understand. I got carried away by all this.' Hannah gestured around them with a wide sweep of her hand. 'Don't worry, I won't say a word.' She covered her mouth and mumbled behind her fingers before pulling them away. 'That was 'my lips are sealed' in case you didn't guess.'

Jack burst out laughing, unable to help himself. 'Fair enough.' He held out his hand and they shook on it. 'You'd better follow me back into Trewarne. I'm assuming you don't want to be seen with me looking like this so, you'll need to hang around in the bar while I shower and change before we can go eat.'

'Might be a good idea.' Her amused gaze swept down over him and she wrinkled her nose.

'The pub where I'm staying has pretty decent food. I hope that'll work for you, because I've got a lot of paperwork and phone calls to do tonight and can't take the time to go far.' He guessed he might sound rude but needed to make it perfectly clear this wasn't a date in the normal sense of the word.

'Perfect. I'll still have to get back home to Torpoint afterwards, so I don't want to be late either.'

Jack crossed his fingers that Gemma wouldn't be working behind the bar tonight. The last thing he needed was to face her again after their earlier run-in. Although if she were to spot him with an attractive woman . . .

7

With her hands plunged in the hot, soapy dishwater, Gemma smiled as laughter drifted in through the half-open kitchen door. She'd insisted on doing the dishes herself when April and Harry got into a friendly argument about who was the ultimate superhero, Superman or Batman. April was a Superman girl through and through, while Harry's love of Batman went all the way back to the first Halloween costume he wore to a school party when he was five.

She finished up and dried off her hands, making a quick decision to leave the wet dishes to dry by themselves for once. Then she stuck the kettle on to boil, but didn't immediately go into the other room. Through the crack in the door she spied April with her shoes kicked off, lying back in one corner of the sofa and looking more relaxed than Gemma had seen her in ages. Harry sat opposite her, his animated face full of mischief as he teased April about having a thing about Henry Cavil's muscles rather than his acting ability as Superman. Gemma wandered in just as April leaned over and poked Harry's arm.

'You're awful, Harry Sommerby,' said her friend, 'and I don't know why I listen to your nonsense.'

Harry froze and reached up to touch his head, the way Gemma had seen him do thousands of times when he was struggling to remember something. He suddenly grasped hold of April's hands. 'Candyfloss. You love pink candyfloss. And the crispy, scrunched-up bits at the bottom of the bag from the chip shop. You hate bullies.' His voice cracked. 'I used to call you my . . . ' He shook his head wildly as if desperate to shake everything back into place.

Gently April stopped him by resting her hand on his cheek. 'Sugarpuff,' she whispered, and as a slow smile crept back across Harry's face Gemma let out the breath she'd been holding. She didn't dare to move or speak.

'Did I love you?' The heartbreaking question filled the room, and Gemma had never felt so sorry for her friend. This was all her own fault. She shouldn't have stirred things up that were best left alone.

'Yes, Harry, you did,' April said in a quiet, matter-of-fact voice.

Harry frowned and tried to speak, stumbling over his words and trying over and over again until Gemma ached to plead with him to stop; to tell him it didn't matter and to forget it. But April waited calmly with a patience she herself could never have had.

'And you loved me back,' he said. The simplicity of his words tore at Gemma, and she couldn't imagine what this was doing to her best friend. So much for her plan to have nothing more than a fun, gossipy evening with too much wine.

'Yes, Harry, I did.' April sat up straighter, and when she spoke again Gemma caught the edge of steel in her voice. 'You were always my good friend. I love all my friends.'

He let go of April's hands but kept his gaze focused on her. 'I have to think some more about this, and you know that's a challenge for me.'

'Write it down in your notebook,' Gemma piped up, and they both stared over at her as though neither one had realised she was there. 'Harry keeps a notebook to prompt him about things he wants to remember,' she explained.

'Good idea, Gem.' He reached over to the table and picked up the small black book he was rarely without. Digging a pen out of his pocket, he started to write. It was a slow process, because writing was one of the most difficult things for him, but several minutes later he closed the book with a satisfied sigh and set it back down. 'Okay. Time for pudding, I think. April told me she made my favourite, cherry cheesecake.' He relaxed back on the sofa as if nothing had happened.

'I'll cut you a big slice. Do you want coffee or tea?' April's casual manner wasn't something Gemma could've achieved, and her admiration for her friend skyrocketed.

'Tea, please. No milk or sugar.' He picked up the remote and turned on the TV.

Without saying anything, Gemma returned to the kitchen and waited for April to join her, wondering what on earth they were going to say to each other.

★   ★   ★

Jack had made a prize idiot of himself. Over dinner he'd spelled out to Hannah the fact that he was only here for a few months, never mixed business with pleasure where relationships were concerned, and had just broken up with a long-term girlfriend. She'd laughed so

70

hard he thought she'd fall off her chair, wiping tears from her eyes and taking what seemed like an eternity to quiet back down. Everyone in the bar had stared at them.

'I'm sorry. Did I give the impression I fancied you?' she said. 'I never meant to. No offence, but you're not my type.'

He hadn't dared to ask what type she'd marked him down as, suspecting the answer wouldn't be flattering.

'I'm engaged and getting married at Easter. My ring is being altered at the moment, so that's why I'm not wearing it today.'

Jack's bruised ego didn't care for the way she'd found the idea so amusing, probably because it wasn't the reaction he got from most women. Gemma pushed her way back into his mind, making things worse. She'd declare it served him right because he was far too cocky and sure of himself.

They'd wrapped up the evening pretty quickly afterwards, and Hannah had sworn it was all forgotten when Jack apologised again. 'I'm sure we'll work together just fine if you decide to choose my company,' she said.

It left him with a huge problem. After his mistake today, he'd prefer they didn't choose Unique Restoration, but that wasn't being fair. If they did give her the job, would Hannah think it was because of his lingering embarrassment? Nothing was ever straightforward.

After he watched her drive away, he didn't rush to go back inside. He found himself unable to face either returning to the bar or working alone in his room. There was an autumnal chill in the air, but he quickly ran upstairs to grab a sweater before strolling down towards the harbour. He leaned in over the old stone wall and stared out over the still, dark sea.

'Jack?'

He turned around, and Gemma's tentative smile glowed in the reflection from the nearby street lights.

'I came out for a walk to clear my

head,' she explained.

'I hope it works.' He didn't have a clue how best to respond after the way she'd shot him down earlier.

'Me too.' Shuffling her feet, she wrapped her arms around herself, and it took all Jack's self-control not to offer to warm her up with a hug. 'I was rude to you this afternoon and I'm sorry. I've had an . . . unusual evening, and it's made me see I've been a coward about a lot of things.'

Jack desperately wanted to avoid putting his foot in it again. Something deep in his gut urged him to make an effort to gain her respect, even if that was all he could have.

'I'd like to take you up on your offer,' Gemma declared, and a deep blush heated her cheeks. Her fair, lightly freckled skin always revealed her emotions as clearly as if she'd shouted them out loud.

'You want to talk?'

'Yes.' Her snappy, defensive retort amused him.

Jack touched her arm in a gesture of reassurance but she flinched, backing away. 'Sorry,' he said. 'I didn't mean to . . .'

'No, it's my fault. Ignore me.'

I wish I could. The same way I wish I could ignore your beautiful mouth. And the delicate scent you use, the same one my memory has held on to all these years. 'Would you like to go somewhere now?' he ventured to ask.

'I suppose we might as well.'

'It's your choice.' Jack was confused. She'd approached him, but now appeared to be regretting it.

'I know.' She gave a heavy sigh. 'Right. Not the Green Dragon, for obvious reasons. The Welly is too noisy, so it'll have to be the Bottoms Up wine bar. It's tucked away in the middle of High Lane around the corner from the post office. It's relatively new and should be quiet. The local tearaways aren't into tapas and chardonnay.'

'You surprise me.' When a glorious smile lit up her face, Jack felt like a child given a brand-new bike on Christmas Day. 'Lead the way.' He wasn't stupid enough to take hold of her hand, although he desperately wanted to. At seventeen it'd taken him five long excruciating dates before he'd dared to try, and when he finally plucked up the courage she'd laughed and asked why he'd waited so long.

'I didn't think to ask if you had anything else planned,' she said. Her reticence had returned, and Jack decided he'd been cautious long enough. He firmly grabbed her elbow and steered her across the road.

'No I don't, or I'd have told you. I'm not going to bite, Gemma.' He smiled. 'I had a good meal earlier.' He loosened his grasp. 'Come on.'

Without another word she kept going, and they made their way slowly through the quiet streets. Jack had never been in Trewarne out of the main tourist season before and found himself liking the sense of a place settling back into its comfortable, ordinary ways.

'There it is.' Gemma pointed to a plain wooden sign sticking out from a narrow building between a sailing shop and another selling handmade Celtic jewellery. She tugged on the heavy iron knob to open the door, and as she stepped inside she warned Jack to mind his head. Unfortunately she said it at the precise second when his skull made contact with the solid oak beam. He cursed and stumbled in after her.

'Sorry,' he mumbled, rubbing at his head.

Gemma stifled a laugh. They'd got off on the wrong foot when he appeared in her shop, and things hadn't improved the second time they met. When she'd noticed him standing by the wall a few minutes ago, she'd been painfully aware of the stiff set of his broad shoulders and the tension radiating from him. She'd fled the house for a while, needing to think. April had refused to discuss Harry, saying it was between the two of them. Gemma had guarded her brother since their parents died and wasn't sure how she felt about him having a private life apart from her. Maybe she should've been more careful what she wished for.

'Are we going to sit down, or would you prefer to stand around and get in the way?' Jack asked.

'We'll sit of course.' Gemma resented the implication that she might've changed her mind again. Glancing around the almost empty room, she spotted a table over by the fire. 'Let's sit there. It's chilly tonight.'

'Years ago you laughed and called me soft when I complained about the frigid temperature of the seawater,' Jack said. 'You'd stay in until your skin turned a very attractive shade of purple complete with goose bumps. No wonder I fell for you.'

His teasing, easy manner loosened something inside Gemma and she laughed along with him. 'And I thought it was my brilliant brain and stunning good looks.'

In the candlelight, his green eyes narrowed. 'Oh it was all that, and more.' The hitch in his voice made her heart flip, the way it'd always done around this man.

'What can I get you two tonight? Here's the wine list, and the specials are on the back.' The cheerful waiter thrust a leather-covered menu at each of them, getting out his notepad and a pen ready to write down their order.

Gemma prayed the dim lighting hid her flaming face and hoped Jack would manage to answer before the waiter decided they were a pair of mutes.

'A bottle of number twelve.' Jack glanced at her. 'An Australian shiraz. Will that suit you?'

She nodded without any clue what she'd agreed to. It could be rat poison for all she knew. All she wanted was to be on their own again and find out exactly what he'd meant by his enigmatic comment.

'Right away, mate.' The waiter took

their menus and disappeared back to the bar.

Gemma rested her elbows on the table and fixed her gaze on Jack. 'I think you've got some explaining to do.'

8

The diffidence written all over Jack's face eased the tight knot in Gemma's stomach — the one that'd been there since he'd walked back into her life. Not that she couldn't appreciate the strikingly good-looking man he'd turned into — she wasn't a complete idiot — but this new hint of vulnerability put him more on her level.

'I'm not sure what you want from me,' Jack murmured as he fiddled with the cardboard coaster.

'I don't *want* anything,' she declared, not sure she was telling the complete truth. 'You. Me. The past. Wasn't that how you phrased it when you said we needed to 'sort this out'?'

He shifted back in the chair and stretched out his long legs, apologising when he accidentally kicked one of her feet under the table. He shoved a hand up through his immaculate jet-black hair, mussing it up, but only making it more attractive from where she sat. Less perfect. More the real Jack Watson.

'I was talking through my head that day,' he said. 'You were right. It's in the past and that's where we should leave it.'

Nothing about his cool, deliberate words rang true. Gemma had enough built-up annoyance inside her to persist, but the waiter reappeared so she held back from replying. He fussed around, offering the wine for Jack to taste before pouring out two glasses and leaving.

Gemma drank deeply, savouring the rich heady wine and tucking away in a corner of her mind what an improvement it was on the bottle of cheap plonk she and April had laughed about earlier. 'Very nice,' she commented.

'So, are you good with that?'

'I said the wine was nice.'

Jack snorted. 'You know I'm not

talking about the wine, Gemma.'

'Answer one question.' A wary look came into his eyes and she knew she'd have to choose carefully if he wasn't going to politely shut down again. 'We were young. I can understand things seeming different when you got back to London, but would it have killed you to at least reply to one of my letters?' She bit the inside of her cheek to stop from crying. She'd done enough of that for months after he'd left.

'Letters? I never got any letters.' The shadowy light caught and magnified the sharp planes of his face, emphasising his confusion. 'I assumed you'd forgotten me.' His voice trailed away, and Gemma instinctively reacted before she could think to hold back.

'I *never* forgot you. Never.'

'Oh, Gemma,' he groaned and reached for her hands, wrapping them with his own, which were solid and warm. 'I'm not that boy anymore. I can't be him for you.'

She nodded, wishing she could brush

away the tears leaking down her cheeks. Instead he did it for her, his touch so swift and gentle it might've been only in her imagination. 'The idealistic, light-hearted girl you knew is long gone too,' she said.

'What changed her?'

What didn't? Him. Losing her parents. Harry. Leaving behind her dreams of a life far from Cornwall. 'Life, Jack,' she eventually said. 'Just life.' She left it there. Burdening him, or anyone, with her regrets wasn't Gemma's way. Her philosophy was to deal with the reality of her life and not look back. 'What changed *you*?'

He shifted in the chair, swirled around the wine in his glass, and pretended to check out the painting on the exposed brick wall next to him. Her question could take a week to answer, even if he was prepared to be truthful. He didn't dare to look at Gemma. She'd always had the uncanny ability to see right through him. 'I could answer the same way,' he said.

83

'You could indeed. Would it be the truth?'

He shrugged. 'Pretty much.'

'How about something easy?' Gemma urged. 'Why the American accent, and what are you doing poking around West Dean House? Satisfy my curiosity on those things at least.'

Jack relaxed and allowed himself to turn his attention back to her. Big mistake. Her mouth curved in a teasing half-smile, and her soft grey eyes danced with mischief. He'd almost forgotten how much fun they'd had together all those years ago, and the way she'd always been able to wheedle things out of him — everything from his crush on Kylie Minogue to admitting the difficult relationship he had with his overbearing father.

'After several jobs in London I was offered a position with Von Doorsten Industries in Nashville, Tennessee,' he explained. 'I've been there about ten years now, and I was recently made a vice president of the company.'

'What do you actually do?'

He grinned. 'That's a great question and hard to answer. I'm Paul Von Doorsten's personal aide and work on projects that fall outside the regular scope of the other VPs. It's challenging, but I love the variety.'

'Goodness. It sounds impressive.'

Jack couldn't decide if Gemma was genuinely amazed or sending him up. He'd become accustomed to behaving in the more overtly confident American way, something that could be perceived as boasting. His father would slam him down if he heard him talking this way.

'What's wrong?' Gemma asked him.

Jack started as she touched his hand, and he met her dark, worried gaze with surprise. 'Nothing. Why?'

'You suddenly went very quiet.' She frowned. 'I didn't mean to mock you. I'm genuinely pleased you've done so well.'

For a second he came very close to being honest with her, but he'd come through the last twenty years by relying solely on himself and it'd served him well — on the surface, anyway, which was the only place he dared to look most of the time.

'No problem. I've had a long day. Guess I ought to be turning in soon.' He knocked back the rest of his wine. 'More?' He lifted up the bottle and refilled his own glass when she refused. 'West Dean House is a tricky subject.'

'I didn't mean to put you on the spot.' Gemma's face heated and he didn't think it was simply a side effect of the wine.

'Let's just say I'm in charge of renovating the house for . . . a client.' He squeezed her hand. 'I wish I could say more but I can't. It means I'll be here until the New Year.' The flash of pleasure he glimpsed in her dark eyes was swiftly replaced by concern. Despite his misgivings, he longed to find out more about this new version of the girl he'd fallen head over heels in love with and never quite got out of his head. Then he could put her behind him for good. *Or is that wishful thinking?* he wondered. He said aloud, 'I hope we can do this again.'

'Why?' The blunt question took him aback and for a minute he didn't respond.

'I could do with a friend,' he said simply, the truth of it surprising him. In Nashville his busy life left little time for introspection, and as an extremely eligible bachelor he didn't have to be alone any more than he chose to be. Cornwall was stirring up more memories than he'd expected. 'How about you?'

Could she ever simply be friends with the handsome man with troubled green eyes staring at her across the table? Gemma doubted it, but couldn't turn down the offer to spend time with him. She'd never been able to say no to Jack Watson, and the fact she was nearly forty and should know better changed nothing. When she told April to throw out the Cinderella fantasy where she and Jack were concerned she'd meant every word, but deep down she suspected she'd never give up the corner of her heart where his name was etched.

'I have almost no free time, Jack, but if you don't expect too much it's fine by me.' She spelled it out as plainly as she could without being rude.

He suddenly reached over and played with a handful of her curls. 'You always had such spirit.' He dropped his hand away and picked up his wine glass. 'Don't worry. My expectations are low.' Raising the glass, he silently toasted her before tossing back the rest of his wine.

For some reason, his dejected words upset Gemma and she wished she could take back her cool response, but it was for her own protection. He'd broken her heart once and she couldn't allow it to happen again.

She unhitched her handbag from the back of the chair. 'I need to get home. Harry will wonder where I've got to.'

'Of course.' He inclined his head and quickly stood up, walking around the table to pull back her chair. 'I'll pay and meet you outside.'

'Let me . . . '

'No, Gemma.' He shook his head. 'At least let me do this.'

She hadn't meant to insult him, but plainly that was how he'd taken her attempt to split the bill. 'Thank you,' she said with as much grace as she could muster. Without saying anything more, she left him and wended her way out through the closely arranged tables. Outside, the cold, damp air soothed her burning face, and she exhaled a huge sigh.

'You're shivering.' Jack's broad hand rested on her shoulder as he stepped out to join her. Out of instinct she snuggled closer, and didn't object when he wrapped her in a warm hug. No one had held her this way for a long time. Actually, never. Naturally she'd had boyfriends since Jack, but no one else made her feel so totally alive and wonderfully secure. Her head rested against his chest, allowing the soft wool of his sweater to brush against her cheek. 'Warm sunshine and lilacs,' he said. 'You still smell wonderful.'

'Don't,' she pleaded, pulling away. 'Friends, you said.'

Under the glow of the moon, Jack's strained expression deepened. 'I did, didn't I.' He idly traced his finger along her jawline, then dropped his arm back to his side. 'More fool me.'

Silence swirled in the air around them, broken only by a lone seagull's raucous cry from the nearby rooftop. Eventually Jack said, 'I'll walk you home.'

Gemma didn't try to argue but walked away without another word. He fell in beside her, not quite touching but close enough that she couldn't help but be aware of his presence. They continued in silence all the way to her house. Outside the gate she turned to thank him, but before she could speak he wished her a curt good night and strode off.

Gemma watched his tall, retreating figure and wondered how she was going to survive until January.

9

All week Jack's pending visit to his parents lingered at the back of his mind, like a sore place on the skin that wouldn't heal. Now he sat in his parked car one street over from their house, trying to make himself drive the last hundred metres. About ten years ago he'd gone to see them in an effort to give their strained relationship one last chance, but his plan to move to America had inflamed his father. The vicious words they'd exchanged were carved deep into Jack's heart. His mother had pleaded with them both to stop arguing, but stubbornness ran deep in their veins and neither would back down.

His father always made it clear Jack was a disappointment, and nothing he did was ever good enough. Praise was only grudgingly given out and was always accompanied with a caveat to make sure he didn't get too cocky and sure of himself. He was never allowed to forget the financial sacrifices his parents had made to send him to the right kind of school, with the idea he'd follow in his father's footsteps to Sandhurst. When Jack had given his father a letter from the school music teacher saying he should consider a professional singing career, Philip Watson's eyes had turned ice-cold; he tore up the letter, tossing the pieces on the floor. 'Music?' he'd shouted. 'What a load of rubbish. You'll go to Sandhurst. It'll make a man of you.'

After a bitter row, Jack's mother had intervened, and as a compromise Jack was sent to university to study business. But his father never forgave him, and in return Jack could never forgive him for trampling his dreams into the dirt.

And now he had to face the man again, keep his temper in check, and somehow get through the afternoon without another row. He started the car back up and slowly made his way down the road, then pulled into an empty parking space outside the house and got out quickly before he could change his mind.

Jack smoothed a hand down over his hair; not regulation army length, but respectable enough. He'd rejected the idea of wearing a suit and instead chose dark brown cord trousers and a muted green and brown checked shirt matched with brown leather shoes he'd spent extra time polishing. His stomach churned due to a mixture of nerves and the fact he hadn't been able to eat any lunch. He reached into the back seat and lifted out the flowers he'd bought for his mother — an extravagant bunch of her favourite white roses — then locked the car and walked towards the house. But before he could press the bell, the door was jerked open.

'You came.' His father checked him out, his sharp green eyes giving Jack's appearance a disapproving once-over.

'I said I would.' Jack was disconcerted to notice that Philip's always-erect military stance was marred by a slight stoop, and his once jet-black hair was steel-grey and thinning.

'Your mother's waiting.' The implication that he was late resonated through the crisp, well-chosen words. Jack said nothing, because defending himself always led to arguments. 'She doesn't care to talk about her illness, so don't ask.'

'Is it serious?'

'Would I have let you back in the house if it wasn't?' Philip scoffed and strode off, clearly expecting his son to follow.

Jack hadn't grown up in this house, as his parents had moved to Plymouth after his father's retirement. The family had followed Philip around with his many postings, and the last time they all lived together was in London when Philip did a succession of hated desk jobs. The magnolia paint and regular furnishings in this house were probably the same as any other three-bedroom semi in the area. Everything was well-maintained, clean but largely forgettable, exactly the way Philip preferred his surroundings. But Jack smiled to himself when he spotted the flowers on the hall table — bright red daisies arranged in one of his mother's garish Sicilian jugs, which was shaped like a chicken. Philip had never quite erased his wife's continuing love for the exuberant colours of her home country, and for that Jack was glad.

He sucked in a few deep breaths before fixing on a smile and walking into the lounge. Keeping the smile in place took every ounce of determination he possessed when he saw his mother, Maria. A shadow of the vibrant woman he remembered, she attempted to rise from the chair to greet her son, but her thin hands failed to grip onto the arms and she immediately fell back into the seat.

'Oh, Jack, I didn't think I'd see you again.' Her voice trembled, and quiet tears trickled down over her papery skin.

His heart split in two and he couldn't have replied if someone paid him a million pounds. Hurrying over, he bent down to hug her, his throat choked dry with overwhelming emotions he didn't know how to express. Her familiar lavender scent teased his nostrils and he bit back tears. He'd been a fool. Punishing his father was one thing, but he'd made a huge mistake with his brash certainty that it'd be easier for his mother if he stayed away. For the first time in his life, he wanted to thank his father for forcing him to do something.

'Stand up so I can see you properly,' she urged, and he instantly complied. 'Such a handsome boy. I can't believe a nice young lady hasn't snatched you up by now.'

He murmured something about his busy job and travelling a lot, implying a much livelier social life than he actually had the time and energy for.

'Philip, would you mind getting the

tea? I'd like to talk to Jack.'

He caught a shadow of his father's sadness etched into his stern features, guessing his mother's request was a euphemism for the fact she wasn't well enough to get the tea ready herself.

'Of course.'

Once they were alone, Jack sat down next to his mother and offered her the roses he'd brought.

'They're beautiful.' Maria stuck her nose in the bouquet to smell the flowers and then laid them carefully on the table. 'Your father tells me you're working in Cornwall.'

Without giving too many details, Jack chatted about West Dean House, knowing she'd enjoy hearing about the plans and hoping it'd help avoid any tougher questions she might dare to ask. 'The renovation should be wrapped up by the New Year,' he said.

'I'd love to see it.' She sighed. 'I suppose you'll return to Nashville then?'

'I plan to.'

'Pity.' The single word got to him and he swallowed hard, trying to think of a soothing reply, but there wasn't one he could give without lying.

'Tea's ready. Make room on the table, son.' His father bustled back into the room, wielding a large tray. Jack couldn't imagine how they were managing, because Philip and domesticity were polar opposites, but he knew better than to ask or sympathise.

'Yes, sir.'

For an hour they drank weak tea and ate a shop-bought sponge cake that his father would never have allowed in the house in the old days.

'I ought to be going,' said Jack eventually. 'I've things to get ready before the builders arrive in the morning.' That was sort of true, but he couldn't bear to sit there any longer. He stood up and leaned in to kiss his mother.

'Come again,' she pleaded.

'I will.'

'Your mother always rests at this

time of day. I'll see you to the door,' his father declared, and a flare of anger surged through Jack. Clearly he couldn't wait to get rid of him.

Kissing his mother one more time, Jack walked out of the room, and would've left without saying another word if Philip hadn't slapped a hand on his shoulder, stopping him in his tracks.

'I'll let you know when to come again.' His terse words didn't match the deep pain in his eyes.

Jack wasn't sure what made him do it, but he held out his hand. 'Thank you for inviting me, sir.' He was sure Philip would refuse to shake his hand, but instead he clasped it and held on for several long seconds before letting go.

'Drive safely.' His father's gruff instruction cut through Jack more than any overt display of emotion.

He nodded and walked away, not daring to look back.

★ ★ ★

'Gemma, do you think it'd be all right if I ask April to go and see the new Superman film with me?' Harry glanced down at his feet, staring at the new trainers they'd bought at the market last week. 'I've been doing a lot of thinking.' Gemma almost made a flippant comment, but held her tongue. 'More stuff is coming back, Gem. Why didn't you tell me she'd been my girlfriend?'

Because I wanted to protect you. I hate it when you're hurting, and I thought this was the safest way. April agreed. At least, I thought she did. Gemma shrugged because she didn't have an answer that he'd understand. *You're supposed to love him. He deserves better than your pity.* She always resented people who jumped to conclusions about Harry, but maybe she'd done it herself by shielding him too much.

'You're good to me, Gem. I know sometimes I get . . . upset when I can't remember things, but I really want to remember April, even if it's tough.' His complete honesty floored her.

'Don't be surprised if she refuses you.' Gemma needed to spell it out. At least then he couldn't turn around afterwards and say she should've warned him.

'Because Mrs. Broad doesn't like me?'

She nodded. 'I love April dearly, but she's never been able to stand up to her mother about anything important. Mrs. Broad likes having her daughter at home, working in the fudge shop, and at her beck and call.' Gemma hesitated, then plunged right on. 'You weren't good enough for April when you were teenagers, and she certainly won't think you are now.' If he wanted bluntness he was going to get it.

Harry frowned and opened up his notebook, quickly scribbling down something. 'She called me a hooligan one night when we'd been out on my motorbike. I'd forgotten that.' He broke into a teasing smile. 'She was probably right.'

'I expect she was.' Gemma laughed. 'Go ahead and ask her. At least that way you'll know.'

'Yep. I will.' He walked across the room and picked up the phone from the coffee table, instantly disappearing into the kitchen and closing the door behind him.

Gemma crossed her fingers behind her back, not sure what she hoped her friend's answer would be. Either way, they couldn't go back from this.

'She said yes!' Harry burst back into the room and grabbed Gemma, twirling her around and laughing. 'We're going today on the five o'clock bus. She suggested we get something to eat before a film at a new burger place near the cinema.' He kissed Gemma's forehead. 'Will you be okay on your own?'

Tears pressed at her eyes and she swallowed hard. Harry asking if she'd be all right was a complete turnaround. Normally she was the worried one. 'Of course I will, silly. I'm working tonight anyway. Eight until eleven.' She looked at her watch. 'You'd better get showered and changed.'

A mischievous twinkle made his eyes shine. 'Do girls like that?'

'Most people prefer not to be sat next to someone who's smelly,' Gemma teased. 'Go on with you.'

He hurried off, but Gemma didn't move right away. Her mind whirred like a hamster on a wheel. A myriad of different scenes played through in an endless loop, and most of them ended up with Harry being hurt. She had to admit she hadn't seen him look as happy in forever, and she hated the streak of jealousy creeping through her. She hoped she wasn't a mean-spirited person, but she'd given up so much for Harry — willingly and out of love — and where had it left her? Creeping closer to forty with a nearly bankrupt business and no prospect of a family of her own.

She was usually a glass-half-full sort of person, but tonight all she saw were the dregs at the bottom of the glass with no prospect of a refill.

10

Gemma brushed her hair and scooped it up in a loose ponytail before peering at the dark circles under her eyes with disgust. She rubbed on a smear of concealer but it didn't do much to help.

She'd better not be pestered by any annoying drunks tonight at the Green Dragon or they'd get the sharp side of her tongue. Hopefully Jack wouldn't be around either. She'd managed to stay out of his way since their excursion to the wine bar. Rumours were starting to fly around the village about the renovation work starting on West Dean House, but she'd made a point of staying well out of it. Wild speculation ranged from the house being purchased by either a wealthy oil sheik or a famous actor who was being hounded by the press.

The cheerful red lipstick Gemma

applied only made her look paler, so she added a layer of blusher to her cheeks — and was instantly horrified at her doll-like reflection in the mirror. She wiped it all off in frustration and made do with a quick slick of her usual pink lip gloss. Glancing at the bedside clock, she realised it was time to go, and ran downstairs to throw on her coat. She picked up her battered tan leather handbag, the same one she'd hauled around for years, and ran out of the door.

'Oh,' she yelped, bumping straight into Jack, who was standing on her doorstep. He stuck out his arm to stop her falling, and flashed his trademark smile. 'What are you doing here?' she asked him.

'That sure isn't a very polite way to speak to an old *friend*.'

'I haven't got time for this. I need to go or I'll be late for work.'

Jack grasped her elbow and his fingers burned through her coat sleeve. 'You can spare me five minutes.'

'I can't afford to. If I'm late Bert will dock my pay.' She glared at him, angry about everything, but especially the way he kept popping up and disturbing her. 'We don't all have fancy jobs and expensive cars.'

He let go of her and backed off. 'Sorry.' He kicked at a stone and muttered something under his breath.

'What did you say?'

Jerking his head up, Jack's sharp green eyes bored into her. 'I didn't mean to be a thoughtless idiot. Something about being back here and around you rattles me.' The blast of honesty shocked her, and judging by how pale he'd gone, Gemma guessed he hadn't intended to say the words either.

'Walk with me, Jack.' She slipped her hand through his arm. 'You won't believe the wild stories flying around the village about West Dean House.' She thought she'd done a smooth job of changing the subject, but by his barely suppressed smile she'd been rumbled.

Why did she always look so fresh and lovely? Jack wondered. When he compared her to the fashionable, well-groomed women he usually dated, in some mysterious way she always came out on top. He guessed Gemma's natural beauty was pretty much effortless, because she didn't have the time or money for it to be anything else.

'Stop staring at me,' Gemma protested. 'Come on. A tortoise could walk faster than you.' She pulled on his arm.

Jack didn't try to explain himself because she'd only laugh. Instead he launched into a light-hearted story about the progress on West Dean House. The roof was fixed and the basic electrical work was done. 'Since yesterday I'm staying there full-time,' he said.

'Really?'

'Yeah. The plumbers worked enough of their magic to get a functioning bathroom for me and running water in the kitchen. It's better than my room at the pub.' He hurried to explain his preference for quiet so she didn't jump on him for insulting the Green Dragon.

They carried on walking as far as the post office before all of a sudden Gemma stopped. 'Why were you lurking outside my house?'

'Lurking? That sounds . . . menacing.' Her cheeks flamed and he quickly stamped on the almost irresistible urge he had to kiss her. 'I wanted to see you. Is that so hard to understand?' He didn't mean to put her on the spot but was tired of tiptoeing around. He'd done enough of that today.

She shrugged. 'I suppose not.'

Not exactly the last word in enthusiasm, but he wasn't about to give in yet. 'What time do you finish tonight?'

'Eleven. But — '

'I'll be here to walk you home.'

'You don't need to do that,' she protested.

'I know I don't. But I want to.' He touched her chin, tilting it up to meet his smile. 'Is that a problem?'

'Fine. Do what you like.' She sighed. *What did you think she was going to* do? Jack asked himself. *Throw herself at you? Ask where you'd been? All of the above?*

'What are you going to do with yourself until eleven?' Gemma asked him.

Jack hadn't planned that far ahead. He just needed to talk to someone before he went crazy. *No. You need to talk to Gemma. It's a completely different thing.*

'Come in and play a game of darts or something,' Gemma suggested, her mouth twitching. 'Do smooth, wealthy Americans even play darts?'

He stepped closer and slid his hands around her waist, pulling her up against him. 'The smooth part is only surface, Gemma. Yes, I'm wealthy. Sorry if that bothers you, but I can't do much about it. I've still got my British passport and a green card, so I'm not strictly American.' He whispered in her ear, 'And we've played enough games for you to know I always win.' The flare of heat colouring her fair skin told him his

110

words struck home, and he pressed a soft kiss on her mouth before letting go. He rubbed his finger over her top lip. 'The same cherry lip gloss. Nice.' He gave in to a lazy smile. 'You go on. I'll be in soon.'

Gemma touched her mouth and seemed about to say something, but then turned away and pushed open the pub door before disappearing inside. Jack let out a long exhalation and wondered what he'd just started. *Started? It never stopped. Get real.* Real. That was exactly how he'd describe Gemma, and why he couldn't stay away.

★ ★ ★

It was like being fourteen again and having her first crush. Gemma remembered sneaking longing glances at Tony Martin in the church choir and making any excuse to go to his father's butcher's shop, where he worked after school.

111

She struggled to concentrate on customers' orders, but all her awareness centred on the dark-haired man laughing and joking with a group of locals around the dartboard. He'd taken her at her word. His easy manner and the fact that he'd bought the first round of drinks did the trick, but she could tell from the cheers and raucous remarks coming from the other men that Jack could actually play. Gemma didn't know why she was surprised. He'd been good at everything he tried, although she'd always sensed his surprise as though his self-confidence was only skin-deep. She'd got the impression his father was a hard man who didn't cut Jack any slack.

'How's the prettiest barmaid in the whole of Cornwall?'

Andy Greenslade. Yuck. Gemma fixed on a smile. The ruddy-faced local postman was a nuisance she could've done without. Most evenings he was a fixture in the bar, convinced he was God's gift to women despite all evidence to the contrary. 'What're you having tonight?' she asked him.

'A pint of Tribute and a kiss, my 'andsome.'

Gemma didn't respond and simply poured his drink and pushed it across the bar.

Andy smirked and held out a five-pound note. 'You can keep the change if I get that kiss.'

'I'm not desperate,' she joked, trying to jolly him along. Suddenly he made a grab for her and Gemma was engulfed by pungent wafts of the cheese and onion crisps he'd been eating. She tried to wriggle from his grasp but it only made him tighten his hold on her shoulders.

'The lady doesn't want to be mauled, so I suggest you let go or I'll do it for you.'

Glancing over Andy's shoulder, Gemma met Jack's green eyes, which were glittering with barely suppressed fury. 'Andy's no trouble. We're fine. Aren't we?' She silently pleaded with her awkward customer to heed Jack's warning before things got nasty. Dealing with people who'd had a little too much to drink, and especially flirtatious men, was part of the job, and she didn't need Jack riding in on his white horse to rescue her.

'Mind your own business, mate,' Andy said, glaring at Jack. 'Gemma's always up for a bit of fun. Not much fun stuck home with your daft brother, is it, love?'

His cruel words stunned her into silence.

'That's it. Clear off now or I'll throw you out.' Jack's harsh tone made it clear he meant what he said. Gemma sighed with relief as Bert ambled out from around the bar and put his hand on Andy's shoulder.

'Come on, pal, time you were going home. I can't afford to have you upsetting my staff.' Firmly he steered the other man out through the crowded bar and into the street before coming back in.

'It's okay. I've got you.' Jack's voice penetrated the fog in Gemma's brain and she was vaguely aware he'd come in around behind the bar and was holding her up. 'Bert, all right if I take Gemma home?'

'I'm fine,' she protested.

'No probs,' Bert assured them. 'Take care of her.' He patted Gemma's arm. 'Don't you take no notice of Andy. Your Harry's a good bloke.'

Nodding through a haze of tears, Gemma managed to pull herself together enough to unhitch her coat from the pegs on the wall and retrieve her handbag from where she'd stashed it back by the till. Jack waited patiently and took hold of her arm when she was ready.

'Come on, love. Let's go.'

They walked along quietly until they reached her house.

'I suppose you're wondering what they meant about Harry?' There was no point ignoring what'd been said.

'I'd be a liar if I said no, Gemma, but you can tell me as much or as little as you want.' Jack's kindness shook the tears loose and she broke down, sobbing into his solid, warm chest. 'Shall we go inside?' he suggested.

Even in her upset state, Gemma realised the significance of his question. Saying yes would be her tacit acceptance that he was more to her than simply an old friend. The trouble was, she didn't know if she could open up her heart to him for a second time. Meeting his frank, steady gaze, there was only one answer she could give.

11

Please say yes. I need to talk to you just as much as I think you need to talk to me. Jack sagged with relief as she slowly nodded her head.

'You'll have to let go of me so I can get my key out.' A tiny smile pulled at her mouth and he glanced down to discover he was clasping Gemma's hands.

'Yeah, sorry.'

'It's okay.' She touched his cheek. 'I didn't mind.'

'Good, because I plan to do it a lot more.' Gemma's dark grey eyes widened. 'I mean . . . well . . . if you're okay with that?'

'I'm not sure what you're asking, but I'm beat and could do with a good cup of tea.' Gemma's no-nonsense reply stopped his rambling. She opened her handbag and Jack peeked into the top.

She glanced up and batted her long eyelashes. 'Yes, there's a lot of stuff in there, but I know where to find everything.'

'Including the famous keys?'

'Of course.' She returned to her search, shoving her hand down to the bottom of the bag and rooting around. 'Eureka.' She waved an overloaded key ring in his face. Playfully sticking her tongue out, she flounced away up the path as fast as her high heels would allow.

Jack followed behind, unable to resist admiring her neat figure in the gleam of light outside her front door. The moment he stepped inside the house, long-forgotten memories surged into his mind, and for a few seconds he couldn't breathe.

'Nothing much has changed,' Gemma commented as she took off her coat and hung it up on one of the wooden pegs on the wall. 'Are you all right?' She frowned.

'Yeah. It's just . . . all so familiar.'

There was so much he thought he'd banished from his mind, only to have it flung right back at him. Visiting his parents today had stirred up a whole raft of emotions; and now, entering this house where he'd first encountered the strength of a loving marriage and happy family, he was overwhelmed again.

He seized Gemma's hands again and pulled her to him for a gentle kiss. 'I never told you properly how sorry I was to hear about your folks. They . . . meant a lot to me.'

'They loved you too.' Gemma's voice trembled. 'My mum always hoped . . . '

'What?' he whispered.

'That you'd come back. She had the crazy idea we were perfect for each other. She understood we were too young at the time, but was ever the romantic.' Gemma scoffed, but Jack sensed a lack of genuine distaste for her mother's dream. A pang of hope mixed with fear shot through him. 'I think we'd better make that pot of tea,' she murmured and pulled away, although he sensed she was doing it out of common sense rather than because she really wanted to. Was it a good thing one of them could be rational?

Jack let her go and wandered around downstairs while she did her good-hostess bit. Everything was neat and clean, but the well-worn furniture was all the same as he remembered, and the walls could all do with a fresh coat of paint. He guessed there wasn't a lot of spare cash floating around for anything non-essential.

Gemma appeared in the doorway brandishing a loaded tray. 'Are you going to take your coat off and stay a while?'

Jack shrugged off his leather jacket and draped it on the end of the sofa. 'We had a few special times on this thing.' He looked at the green floral fabric and grinned. 'Remember when your dad caught us kissing one night after he thought I'd already gone home?'

'Do I ever.' Gemma rolled her eyes.

'His punishment was to send poor Harry with us on our next three dates. The perfect humiliation.' She sat down and patted the cushion next to her. 'We're grown-ups now. It's safe.'

No, it's not. I've never been safe around you, which is why I love you. Jack mentally slapped himself. Even in his head that was a dangerous statement.

'Milk and sugar?'

Jack started as Gemma poked at his arm. 'Earth to Jack . . .'

'Sorry. Did you say something?'

Gemma gave him a very thoughtful look. 'How do you take your tea?'

Iced and loaded with sugar. After ten years in Nashville he'd picked up the southern habit, but she'd think he was crazy if he suggested such a bizarre thing. 'No milk or sugar, thanks.'

'Chocolate digestive?' Her eyes shone as she held out the plate. 'How you stayed skinny I'll never know. You were a human Hoover. A packet of biscuits wasn't safe around you.'

'I'm more cautious these days.'

'Only about biscuits?'

He shook his head. 'No. Twenty years have hopefully given me a little sense.' He hesitated, not wanting to spoil the fragile bond between them. Resting his fingers on her bare arm, he took a chance. 'Do you want to tell me about Harry?'

Gemma grabbed her tea mug and cradled it in her hands for the warmth. She thought it might be easier not to meet Jack's sympathy head on, so kept her gaze focused on the worn-out carpet and the film of dust on top of the television. As unemotionally as she could manage, she recited the whole story, ending up by explaining where Harry was tonight.

'They should be back soon. I don't want him or April to be hurt. But what can I do?' She sneaked a glance at Jack, and his perceptive green eyes, a unique colour she'd never seen on anyone else, met hers.

'Be there for him,' he answered. 'If he

falls he'll need you, but if he's happy he'll need you then too.' His quiet words struck home and Gemma managed a tiny smile. 'It's all any of us crave from the people who are supposed to love us.' A tinge of bitterness coloured his words.

'You haven't always had that, have you?' Gemma took a stab in the dark, hoping she was wrong. As she wondered if she'd gone too far, he finally spoke again.

'No.'

'You don't have to tell me.' *I want you to, but I won't beg.*

'I want to.' Jack's gruff response hinted at the emotions dragging him down. 'No, that's wrong — I *need* to.' His haunted expression tore at Gemma and she couldn't resist hugging him, relieved when he rested his head against hers.

'Your father?' she asked.

He struggled to answer, and the reverberation of his deep, heaving breaths filled the room.

Suddenly the lounge door was flung open and bounced back against the wall. 'That was an ace film, Gem,' Harry exclaimed, strolling in with a big smile all over his face and dragging April in behind him by the hand. 'Oh. Sorry. Didn't know you had . . . Jack? Jack Watson?'

Jack sprung up from the sofa and stuck his hand out at Harry. Gemma didn't know how he managed it, but no one would guess he'd been on the verge of breaking down a few minutes ago. Something bothered her about the fact he could change so fast.

'Good to see you, mate. How are things?'

Harry beamed. 'Not bad. Could be worse.'

'Do you two want tea?' Gemma asked.

'That would be great,' April said. 'I'll come and give you a hand.' Her shrewd stare made Gemma blush. There wasn't much choice, so she got up and headed back into the kitchen, not daring to look at Jack on her way out.

'So what's up with you and Mr. Handsome?' April teased as she lifted down a couple of mugs from the shelf.

'It's complicated.' It was impossible to know where to start. 'Why don't you tell me how your evening went.'

'Changing the subject won't work for long. We'll come back to your surprise visitor later. To satisfy *your* curiosity, we had a great time.' April's face softened into a shy smile. 'I know this sounds stupid, but I was so afraid it wouldn't be the same.'

'Was it?'

She shook her head. 'No. But I've come to the conclusion different isn't always bad. Harry's quieter and more thoughtful, I suppose because he has to think things through more these days.'

Gemma topped up the tea pot with boiling water and gave it a stir. She picked over her words before she spoke. 'He needs a lot of patience sometimes.'

'I know that.' April scoffed. 'It's not

like we haven't been around each other all this time.' She fetched the jug of milk from the fridge and poured a little into each of their mugs. 'We only went to see a film. Don't make too much of it, Gemma.'

She glanced over, noticing the spots of pink on her friend's cheeks and a new gleam in her eyes. Through all the turmoil of Harry's accident and losing her parents, April was always there for Gemma, and she dared not risk their deeply important friendship by speaking out of turn. She'd bite her tongue and keep her fingers crossed that things would work out.

'Before we go back in there, tell me why Jack's sitting on your sofa, why he looked so upset when we arrived, and why you're as tense as a highly strung racehorse?'

April never did miss much. Gemma quickly decided how much to share and what was best kept to herself. She gave a brief version of her set-to with Andy Greenslade and implied it was the cause of the worry her friend picked up on.

'That's it?' April didn't sound convinced and Gemma couldn't blame her. 'I'll let you get away with it for tonight, but we both know you're not being completely honest.' She picked up the two mugs before disappearing back into the lounge.

Resting against the counter, Gemma pressed her fingers against the growing headache creeping across her temples. Jack had been so close to opening up about his father, something she guessed he might never have done before. But the sliver of opportunity had escaped them now, and she'd sensed his relief. She sighed and plastered on a smile as she prepared to join in the good-humoured conversation drifting in through the half-open door, hoping she could fool them all.

12

Jack thanked his lucky stars that Harry and April had walked in before he made a fool of himself. One rule of life his father ingrained in him was that whining was for losers. You took the hand you were dealt and made the best of it, whether it was on the battlefield or in the boardroom. No looking back. For a few moments Gemma's blatant sympathy almost undid him.

'I need to make a move,' he announced and shifted off the sofa, grabbing his coat and slipping it back on. 'I've got an early start in the morning.'

'Before telling us what you're up to at West Dean House? You're a spoilsport, Jack Watson,' April declared, and he glanced over at Gemma, hoping she'd help him out. By her serene, unfathomable expression he took a wild guess she had no intention of stepping in.

'I'm in charge of renovating it for a client who wishes to remain anonymous for the time being.' The brief, blunt explanation clearly didn't impress April, judging by her screwed-up face. 'Sorry,' he added.

'I'll see you out,' Gemma insisted, and jumped up to join him before he could stop her. She firmly closed the lounge door and walked out into the hall. 'You've changed your mind,' she said. He couldn't deny her accusation, so contented himself with a brief shrug of his shoulders. 'It's eating at you, Jack. Think about it, and if you change your mind you know where I am.'

'And if I don't, that's it with us?'

Gemma's eyes narrowed. 'There is no real 'us', which you'd know if you could be honest for once.' Her wry smile unsettled him. 'Oh, I forgot — you don't do honesty. It was never your favourite thing, and nothing seems to have changed. Pity.'

The calm dismissal of their relationship chilled Jack to the bone, and he struggled to reply.

'You're not messing me around a second time,' Gemma said firmly.

Any attempt to protest would demand explanations that Jack wasn't prepared to give. He rested his hand on Gemma's arm, but she flinched and stepped away.

'I'd hoped things could be different, but I'm pretty sure I was fooling myself.' A film of tears shaded her gentle grey eyes, and Jack hated himself for hurting her again. 'Go, please,' she whispered, pulling open the door and letting in a cold blast of wind as he stepped outside.

'Will I see you again?' he asked her.

'This is a small village. I'm sure we'll bump into each other between now and January.' *In other words, we won't on purpose, but I'll be polite if I see you. Nothing more, nothing less.*

Jack hated leaving this way, but she wasn't giving him any choice. Well, why should she? 'Take care of yourself,' he said.

'Oh, I will. I'm used to doing that.' Gemma closed the door quietly in his face and Jack was left on the step, wondering.

Gemma rested her head against the door and wanted to howl. She should never have let Jack back into her heart, not even one tiny corner. And she had done. Not that she'd ever admit it to him or anyone else. Because she was coming up on forty and still single didn't mean she'd compromise and make do with a half-hearted kind of love. Of course they'd never mentioned the 'L' word this time around, but it had hovered in the air between them. Maybe Jack hadn't experienced it with his parents, but her own showed her what a loving marriage looked like every single day, and she wanted nothing less for herself.

'Is everything okay, Gem?'

Harry's question made her turn around. She wiped her eyes and desperately tried to smile. 'I'm fine. Just tired. It's been a long day.' At least that was the truth. 'I'm going to bed.' She brushed away some loose strands of hair, vaguely aware she probably looked a mess.

'April's in the loo. I'm going to walk her home.'

The casual way he announced his intention pulled at Gemma. There was a new sureness about her brother she hadn't seen since before his accident and it touched her heart. 'Good idea.' She bit back the warning she'd been about to issue. Normally she'd tell him to come straight home and not to respond to any of the loud-mouthed teenagers who hung out around the harbour and sometimes teased him. Having faith that he could cope might take a while, but she needed to make a start. 'Do you have your key so I can lock the door when I go up?'

Harry smiled and pulled his keys out of his pocket. 'All present and correct.' 'Good.'

He placed his hands on her shoulders and kissed her forehead. 'Take care, Gem.'

To be told the same thing by the two men she cared for most brought the tears flooding back, and she blinked hard to force them away.

'You sure you're all right? I can tell you're sad.' Harry touched her chin, lifting her face to his worried gaze. 'The other day you told me I wasn't stupid, so don't treat me as if I couldn't understand.'

'It's not . . . that. It's a girl thing.' She'd learned that one mention of anything female-related usually freaked men out, and predictably, her reply instantly shut Harry up.

He raised his hands and laughed, jokingly backing away. 'Fair enough. Sleep well.'

Gemma trailed back into the kitchen to wash the tea things, hating to wake up in the morning to a messy house. She soon had everything straight, and dried her hands before hanging the tea towel up to dry.

April popped her head in around the door. 'Good night. Get some sleep. You need it.'

Obviously Gemma's attempt to cover up her miserable mood had failed. 'Thanks.' The touch of sarcasm was lost on her friend, who waved and disappeared, still smiling broadly.

Gemma heard the front door slam and went back out to lock up for the night. The idea of bed wasn't enticing, but what else was there to do? She dragged herself upstairs and peeled off her clothes before pulling on a warm flannel nightdress. Climbing into bed, she pulled up the layers of mismatched covers and struggled to get warm. She refused to put the central heating on despite the fact that Cornwall in late October was damp and chilly. The electricity bill would be high enough without her being weak-willed about a little cold air.

Earlier in the week she'd pored over the shop accounts, and it'd made depressing reading. The way things looked, she doubted Cornish Treasures would survive the winter. Over breakfast Harry had floated the idea of him trying to get a regular job. She hadn't wanted to burst his bubble of optimism, but in this tough economic climate couldn't see anyone employing him full-time. He often picked up jobs around the village and could turn his hand to pretty much anything, but it wasn't steady enough to depend on where the bills were concerned. And when Jack had asked about Harry's art, she'd avoided answering. As a young man her brother was a talented watercolour artist, but after the accident he'd showed no interest for a long time. One day he'd dug out his paints, but when he couldn't handle the brush without his hand shaking he'd given up. Years later that side of his physical recovery had settled down, but he still rejected her suggestion to give painting another try.

Gemma smiled to herself. A word in

April's ear might do the trick. Harry was no different from any other man when it came to wanting to impress a woman. She snuggled down further in bed and thought she might be tired enough to sleep after all.

★ ★ ★

Through sleep-heavy eyes a loud noise interrupted her dreams, and Gemma struggled awake only to realise someone was banging on the front door. She slipped out of bed, shoving her feet into her sheepskin slippers and reaching for her old purple dressing gown hanging on the back of the door.

Harry. The silly boy had probably lost his keys. She'd brain him for frightening her this way. Gemma hurried down the stairs, tying the belt around her waist as she ran. 'All right, I'm coming,' she yelled, and took the key off the hook. Fumbling with the lock, she got it open and yanked the door back.

'I told you to . . . ' Her voice trailed away at the sight of Steve Penberth's grim face. The community policeman was wearing his uniform and was obviously here on business. Gemma swayed, the blood draining from her face as she heard him say her name.

'It's okay, Miss Sommerby; not totally, but . . . how about I come in out of the cold to talk?'

'Is it Harry?' she whispered, hardly able to spell out her fear.

He touched her arm. 'Yes, but it's not too bad.' Holding on to her, Steve stepped inside and steered her towards the kitchen. He pulled out a chair and gently pushed her to sit down.

Gemma watched in a daze as he crossed over to the sink and filled the kettle before turning it on. He came to sit by her and picked up her hand. 'Harry's in the hospital.' She yelped and tried to get up but he held her still. 'Listen a minute, Gemma.' Gently he explained that Harry had done exactly what she'd come close to warning him against earlier. Near April's house they'd been surrounded by a group of local youths who'd been drinking all evening. They'd started to tease him, and when they'd made fun of April for being with him he told them to mind their language. One of them made a grab for April, and Harry threw a punch at the boy, which fired up the whole gang to set on him. April's screams got the attention of a couple of local people out for a late-night walk with their dogs and they rushed to help. The boys scattered and ran off, leaving Harry unconscious on the ground.

'Oh my God.' She slapped her hand over her face and hot tears ran down her cheeks.

'He looks bad, Gemma, but the doctors say he'll be all right. Do you want to ring someone to take you to Treliske?'

Jack popped into her mind, but she ruthlessly kicked him out. She wasn't going to turn to him after the way he'd rejected her earlier. She shook her head.

'I'll drive myself.'

'Are you sure? I'd take you myself, but I'm on duty.'

'Is April with Harry?'

Steve nodded. 'She went with him in the ambulance and asked me to come and see you.'

The strength of determination that'd got Gemma through so much already returned, and she straightened her spine. 'I promise I'll be fine. I'm going to get dressed and then I'll be on my way.' She stood up and held out her hand. 'Thanks for coming, Steve. I appreciate it.' He shook her hand, not looking at all sure but obviously afraid to push any further.

As soon as she'd seen him out, Gemma hurried back upstairs and refused to let herself think of Harry or anything else while she did what was needed. When she pulled into the hospital car park half an hour later, she clasped the steering wheel tightly, thankful she'd made the drive unscathed.

It seemed ages before she got through all the red tape and barrage of nurses and doctors keeping her from Harry. By now her imagination was running wild; and despite all their assurances that he wasn't seriously hurt, Gemma couldn't bring herself to believe them. The horror of seeing him after the motorbike accident years ago flooded back with a vengeance, and she struggled to keep breathing.

'He's in here.' A short, dark-haired nurse showed her into a semi-private room. 'The ward was full and he'll get a quieter night in here. The doctor will reassess him in the morning.'

Gemma's eyes adjusted to the dim lighting and she spotted April sitting on a chair, leaning over the bed to hold Harry's hand. Gemma crept closer and stifled a gasp. Harry's swollen, bruised face was barely recognisable. 'Oh, my poor love, what've they done to you?'

April's big blue eyes were swimming with tears. 'This is all my fault.'

Gemma knew she should reassure

her friend that she was talking non-sense, but her throat tightened around the lie that wouldn't come out. They stared at each other, and the only sound came from the bleeping machines Harry was hooked up to and the ticking clock on the wall.

13

Jack battled with one contractor after another, and by mid-afternoon he was starving and cheesed off. Ever since last night he'd been beset by Gemma's disdainful face when she'd sent him away. He needed to go and apologise to her. It might not mend their brittle relationship, but at least he'd have a clearer conscience.

Thanks to the useless electrician, the water heater had blown, so his much-needed shower verged on arctic. He shivered as he towelled dry and quickly pulled on a clean pair of black jeans and a warm, dark green wool jumper. He found his black leather jacket and gathered up his wallet and keys, grabbing his mobile as he headed out the front door.

On the way he debated whether to eat first or face Gemma. Seeing her won out, and he managed to find a parking space opposite the shop. Striding across the street, he stopped short at the door when he saw the 'closed' sign in place although it was only three o'clock. He dived into the boutique next door and smiled at the shop owner, who was busy arranging a selection of vividly coloured blouses in the window.

'Excuse me,' he said, 'but do you know why Cornish Treasures is closed?' The middle-aged bleach-blond scrutinised him closely. Jack didn't think he looked suspicious, but plainly she wasn't convinced about his intentions. 'I'm Jack Watson, an old friend of Gemma's,' he explained. He held out his hand and she shook it, albeit a touch reluctantly.

'I'm Mavis Green. You're the American doing up the old West Dean place, aren't you?'

Obviously he wouldn't get anything out of her if he didn't turn on the charm, so he gritted his teeth and went to work. 'I sure am. Are you familiar with the house?'

'My mother used to clean for old Mr. Dean. Funny old chap, he was.'

Jack's interest was aroused. He'd been wanting to find someone with intimate knowledge of the house when it was last in use. 'Is your mother, um, living nearby?' Better than asking outright if she was still alive.

'Yes, she lives with us. She's ninety but you wouldn't know it. Her mind's sharp as a tack and she does the crossword in the paper every day.'

The interior decorators would love to chat to the old woman, Jack mused, but he must tread carefully and not push too hard. Subtly he got the subject around to whether she thought her mother would be willing to chat with him. Her sudden burst of raucous laughter startled him.

'Mother bores us to death talking about the old place,' she said. 'You're welcome to come listen to her. It'll give us all a break.'

Flashing his signature smile, Jack passed over one of his business cards. 'Would you call me when it's convenient?'

'Of course.' She tucked the card into her pocket. 'Look at me rambling on. I forgot what you came in here for in the first place. You were asking about Gemma. The poor girl's with her brother at the hospital in Truro.'

A shiver ran through Jack as Mavis launched into a convoluted story about Harry's run-in with a gang of local hooligans late the previous night. 'They beat him up badly but apparently he'll be all right. Course, the poor chap wasn't good to start with, so I don't know . . . '

Jack forced himself to be polite, though he was longing to run out of there and get to Gemma. 'Thank you so much for your help,' he said. 'I really appreciate it, and I'll look forward to meeting your mother.'

Mavis eyed him up and down. 'So will she when I tell her.'

'I'll leave you to get on.' He made his escape before she delayed him any longer. If he rang Gemma she probably wouldn't answer, so his only choice was to turn up at the hospital and hope she'd be too polite to throw him out.

He stopped at the local garage on the way out of Trewarne to fill up with petrol, and grabbed a couple of chocolate bars and a tin of drink to keep him going. Back in the car he cranked up the radio and concentrated on the road ahead.

* * *

Gemma gingerly held her coffee and hurried down the corridor. *Why do vending machine plastic cups always burn your hand?* She wondered if April would come back to see Harry when she finished work, after the way Gemma had spoken to her last night.

Gemma had been shaken to the core by the sight of her brother motionless in the bed. All that ran through her head was the fact that she couldn't face going through it all again, with the endless months of rehabilitation and not knowing if he'd recover. She had blamed herself because she was supposed to watch out for him. It'd been the last thing her mother asked of her, and she'd failed. She'd turned on April, and the bitter, scathing words she'd thrown out would be hard to take back. Quietly her friend had listened, not refuting anything, and after saying goodnight to Harry she'd gathered up her things and left with a grace that put Gemma to shame.

Pushing the door to Harry's room open, she froze, slopping hot coffee over her hands and onto the floor. 'Ow!' she yelped.

Jack leapt up from sitting by her brother's bed and hurried over to her. 'Are you all right? Give that to me.' He took the cup from her, gesturing at the small sink on the wall. 'Cool off your hands. I'll clean the floor.'

As Gemma held her throbbing hands

under the cold tap, she checked out Jack from the corner of her eye. He cleaned off the outside of the cup and set it on the table before mopping up the spilled coffee.

'Is that better?' he asked her. She nodded and he came back to her, gently holding her hands and turning them over and back again while he examined them carefully. His soothing touch worked wonders and she didn't hurry to pull away. 'You'll live,' he declared, his mouth turning up at the edges in a wry smile. 'I'm sorry if I startled you.'

'If?'

'Okay, guilty as charged. What's my punishment to be?'

She told herself she shouldn't be standing here bantering with Jack after sending him away last night. She withdrew her hands and let them fall back down to her sides. 'I don't know how you found out Harry was here, but thanks for coming.' She spoke with excruciating politeness. 'The doctor says he needs to rest as much as possible, so it'll be better if you leave now.' *For my sanity as much as Harry's recovery*, she added silently.

A dark shadow crossed Jack's face. 'Do the police know who did this to him?' Plainly he wasn't going to take any notice of her request anytime soon. She should've known.

'April recognised a couple of them, and a local man who scared them off knew one other boy. The police are following it all up.' She shrugged. 'They'll probably get community service and a slap on the wrist.'

Jack shook his head and stared back over at Harry. 'Just let me get my hands on them and I'll . . .'

She touched her finger to his lips, begging him to be quiet. 'He can hear us. I don't want him to get upset.'

'Sorry.' Jack shoved his hand up through his hair and his exasperation showed. 'It just gets to me.' His raspy whisper brought tears to Gemma's eyes and his concern for Harry touched her heart. 'Why don't we sit down?' he suggested.

She didn't have the strength to refuse him. He fetched another chair from over by the window and set it next to the bed. Keeping his voice low, he explained that he'd spoken to Mavis Green and come straight to the hospital. 'She said Harry was going to be okay. Is she right?'

Gemma nodded. 'Apparently it looks worse than it is. His eye was swollen shut last night but it's a little better today. At first they thought his nose was broken, but found out it's just badly bruised. He's got a couple of broken ribs but those simply need rest to heal. They're keeping him here for tonight; hopefully he'll be able to come home tomorrow.' Absently she patted Harry's hand. 'He can't talk much because one of those hooligans hit his jaw really hard, so it's still very sore.'

'Thank goodness April was there to call for help.'

'If it wasn't for *her*, Harry wouldn't

have been there in the first place,' Gemma jumped down his throat. 'He could've been killed.' Big, fat tears rolled down her face, and Jack wrapped his arms around her, letting her quietly sob her heart out.

'Shush,' he murmured. 'I hope you didn't say that to her.' A deafening silence hung between them and Jack sighed. 'Oh, Gemma.'

'You don't understand,' she hissed. 'Mum made me accept responsibility for Harry. I've never let her down — until now.'

Harry suddenly tugged at the sheet and struggled to sit up. Jack turned away and rested a hand on his shoulder, patting it gently. 'It's all right, pal. You're okay, and Gemma's here.'

She got up and leaned closer, trying to understand Harry's low mumbles. 'It's so frustrating,' she said. 'I can't tell what he's trying to say. He can't write anything down either, because his hands are too swollen.' She swallowed hard. 'They were hurt when he tried to protect April.'

'Succeeded too. Didn't you, Harry?' Jack's kind words brought the first hint of a smile Gemma had seen to her brother's face since before the fight.

He turned to her. 'Is April coming to visit tonight?'

Her cheeks flamed, and she wasn't certain how to reply.

'Please say you didn't tell her to stay away,' he growled, and she'd never been so ashamed.

'Not exactly.'

'You either did or you didn't,' he persisted.

'I might've said it'd be better if she waits to see you again until we get home,' Gemma muttered.

Harry grabbed Jack's arm. 'April,' he stammered, his weak voice rough with pain. 'Want April.'

'She'll be here soon,' Jack promised. 'Gemma's going to ring her right now and let her know you want to see her.' He glanced back over his shoulder, his thick, dark brows raised in a question.

Between them they had her cornered. Gemma gritted her teeth. 'Of course I will, Harry. I can't use my mobile in here so I'll have to go out in the hall to phone. As soon as I talk to her I'll be right back.'

'No hurry. I'm not going anywhere,' Jack announced and sat back down.

I didn't think you were. She put on a false smile and hurried away. She walked out into the corridor, and as she turned her phone back on someone rushed around the corner and crashed right into her. 'Oh!' She stumbled and almost fell until a steady hand righted her.

'I'm so sorry. Oh, it's you.'

She met April's startled blue eyes and for a second neither of them spoke. 'I came out to ring you,' Gemma said, waving her phone around.

'Really?'

'Yes, really.' She hated apologising. Her mother had been the same way. 'Harry was asking for you,' she mumbled.

'Is he any better?' April frowned and deep worry lines creased her tired, pale face. Plainly she hadn't got any sleep either.

'I suppose so, though he still looks terrible.' Tears filled Gemma's eyes and she broke into loud, hiccupping sobs, feeling a fool. April instantly wrapped her in a tight hug and made soothing noises. 'I'm sorry. So sorry,' she babbled. 'I was frightened. I never meant to blame you. You're good for Harry. He hasn't been this happy in ages.' It was the truth, and now Gemma could acknowledge how grateful she was to her friend for taking a big leap of faith with her brother.

'Nor have I.' April smiled. 'I'm terribly sorry, too. I felt guilty enough over the fight anyway and flipped out at you because I was scared stiff as well. You only said what I was thinking.'

'Jack was horrified when he found out how I'd spoken to you.'

'He's here?'

'Yes.' Gemma couldn't help sighing.

'He found out about Harry and turned up. I can't seem to get rid of the man.' By the way April smirked, it was clear she saw right though the weak protest. 'Let's go. Harry's waiting.'

They linked arms, and Gemma mentally thanked Jack for interfering. Annoying man.

14

'How about I replace the cup of coffee I scared out of you earlier? I spotted a café on the way up here,' Jack suggested. 'We can leave these two on their own for a while.' Gemma's unsmiling face clearly told him the idea didn't thrill her.

'Fine.' She grabbed her handbag and strode out of the room.

Harry grunted, sticking up his bandaged thumb. 'Good luck, pal.'

'He'll need it,' April laughed.

Jack made his way after Gemma and caught up with her halfway down the corridor. He slipped his hand through her arm, forcing her to slow down and walk beside him. 'You're cross with me,' he murmured.

'How very observant of you.' Gemma's clipped reply made it clear he hadn't yet been forgiven for interfering.

She stopped mid-stride and glared at him. 'I'll say this once, and don't expect me to do it again. You were right. Okay. I apologised to April and everything's fine between us now.' She untangled her arm but he instantly slipped his hand around her waist so she couldn't move.

'You've just told me an important thing about you.' He grinned. 'It kills you to say sorry, doesn't it?' He watched the struggle taking place in her, between the dark frown creasing her forehead and the smile pulling at the corners of her mouth. 'It's okay. I don't care for it much myself. Eating crow is never a pleasant experience.'

'It tastes awful.' Gemma's dry words tickled Jack and he burst out laughing. 'Stop it, you horrid man.' The problem was, the more she glared, the harder he laughed until his stomach hurt. 'This café better have a good selection of fattening cakes or you're in even more trouble,' she said.

'Not sure I could be, sweetheart.'

'Oh, trust me, you could,' she retorted. Jack smirked and a fierce blush heated her face and neck. With a dismissive snort she stalked off, leaving him to follow behind, still laughing.

Staying at a safe distance, he found her already sitting in the café at a table for two with her hands folded on her lap. 'I'm not in the mood for coffee,' she told him. 'You can get me a large mug of tea with very little milk and no sugar. I also want a slice of their most expensive chocolate cake. You owe me.' Her dancing eyes softened the blunt order and he couldn't resist kissing her softly on the mouth.

'Yes, ma'am. I am your devoted slave.' The inscrutable look she threw him was disconcerting but he didn't make any comment.

He went up to the counter to order and sensed her watching him all the time he made idle conversation with the lady serving. He loaded up a tray to carry back to the table. 'There you go. One hot tea and one heart-clogging slice of chocolate cake.'

'I would expect my tea to be hot, and at least I'm in the right place if the cake gives me any problems, so be quiet. Drink your coffee and eat your boring fruit scone. By how dry it looks, I'd bet anything it's stale and left over from yesterday.'

'Thanks for the sales pitch. Let's hope they never employ you to promote their food.'

Gemma's jaw tightened. 'Why do you always do this to me?'

Jack held his tongue, having no clue what she was talking about.

'I can be mad as anything with you, but then you turn on the quick-witted charm again and I'm doomed.' She exhaled a long sigh. 'The last thing I need is to get tangled up with you after the way things ended last time. You're only doing a short-term job here and then you'll disappear back to Nashville. I've got a . . . complicated life. I can't go through all this every twenty years. Why can't you leave me alone?'

Her heartfelt plea touched him and he decided to risk something close to honesty. 'I don't know, Gemma. If I did, it might help us both, but I'm as confused as you are.'

'Really?' A tiny smile brightened her worried eyes.

Jack took the mug away from her and set it back down on the table before cradling his hands around hers. His clear green eyes rested on her, and the familiar happy flutter she always experienced when he was anywhere near trickled through Gemma's body.

'Yes, really.' The hitch in his voice told her this wasn't easy for him either. She glanced anxiously around and was relieved to see they were almost alone in the café. The only other customer was an older man staring sadly out of the window and two waitresses who were busy chatting to each other behind the counter. 'Come out to dinner with me tonight,' he said softly. His thumbs rubbed over Gemma's skin, warming it to his touch. 'I want to talk, but this isn't the place.'

'Are you going to chicken out again like you did last night?' She wasn't in the mood to play games, especially after the last twenty-four hours.

Jack slid his right hand up to cup her face, drawing her to him for a gentle kiss. 'No. I've broken enough promises to you. I'm not breaking any more.'

She wanted to believe him, but her innate sense of caution forced her to hold back.

'It's all right. I don't expect you to believe me.' Gemma started at his perceptive comment but didn't reply. 'As they say, the proof of the pudding is in the eating.' His eyes flashed with mischief. 'And from the way you've demolished that cake, I'd say you like eating.' The light touch of humour broke up the moment and Gemma was grateful. Jack was right again. A hospital café wasn't the best place to discuss what was in their hearts.

'You ready to go?' he asked.

'I'd rather sit here with you.' Gemma slapped a hand over her mouth, her skin burning in a furious blush.

'That'd be my preference too, but I thought your responsible-sister gene would kick in soon so I didn't want to push my luck.'

'I hate saying you're right yet again,' she joked, pushing the chair back to stand up. 'Come on.'

This time when they walked back to the ward, Jack wrapped his warm, strong hand around hers and all she knew was that it felt right to be with him again. He'd been her first love, and if she was honest no one else since ever came close to capturing her heart.

She stopped outside the door and peeked in, then bit her lip to stifle a cry of surprise. Harry's and April's heads touched as the latter leaned in over the bed while the former gently stroked her back with his bandaged hand.

'Don't spoil it for them,' Jack whispered in Gemma's ear, his hands circling her shoulders.

'But — '

'Let them work it out. April's a sensible woman, and anyone can see she loves him. It's not a bad start. Harry's a decent man. He deserves this.'

Logically Gemma knew he was right, but that didn't make it any easier to take a step back. 'Maybe I haven't done him any favours. I thought I was protecting him, but maybe he simply went along with it because he felt guilty and didn't want to upset me.'

Jack turned her around to face him. 'Don't assume you know how his mind works.' His lips curled into a teasing smile. 'I suspect Harry would be the first to say he isn't always sure of that himself. When he's better, talk to him and be honest. Talk to April as well. But first let them get through this.'

She nodded and didn't object when Jack let go of her and pushed open the door, moving aside to let her go in first. 'Here we are,' she declared with a bright smile.

'The doctor came in while you were gone,' April said. 'He was pleased with Harry's progress and said he should be discharged in the morning after they do their rounds.' She glanced lovingly at Harry. 'I'm happy to come and pick him up, so you can go ahead and open your shop back up. Mum can do without me for once.'

Jack squeezed Gemma's shoulder and it made her hesitate long enough to think before she spoke. 'If Harry's happy with the plan, it's fine by me. It'd be a big help,' she conceded.

'Thanks, Gem.' Harry's raspy voice was getting stronger. She met his understanding gaze head-on and blinked back tears. He understood how difficult this was for her.

'If y'all don't mind, I'm going to whisk this lovely lady off for a meal,' Jack announced.

Gemma almost protested that visiting hours weren't up yet but held her tongue. After a flurry of goodbyes and promises that Harry would ring if he needed anything, she found herself back out in the corridor with Jack.

'Did you drive here?' he asked, grabbing her hand and steering them towards the exit.

'Yes, but I went home briefly this morning to check on the shop and tell Mavis what was going on, then came back on the next bus. The parking charges here are horrific. I camped out in the waiting room when I wasn't allowed in with Harry.' She put her free hand up to her hair, running her fingers over the tangled mess. 'You didn't tell me I was looking a sight.'

He shrugged. 'I'm not an objective observer. To me you're always beautiful.' Jack's casually tossed-out comment took her breath away. He popped a kiss on her forehead and flashed his signature grin, turning her stomach to mush. 'Now I know how to shut you up if it's ever necessary — simply give you a compliment.'

Gemma was certain there must be hordes of glamorous women throwing themselves at him back in Nashville and couldn't think what he saw in her, but his blatant admiration warmed her all the way down to her toes. 'Do I get to ride in your pretty car?'

'Sorry.' He shook his head. 'I needed something more practical once I established I'd be staying, so I turned the Porsche back in to the rental company and got a sensible four-wheel drive Range Rover instead. I can haul stuff around in that if necessary and it'll be safer if the weather turns nasty.'

Gemma put on a fake grimace. 'I suppose it'll have to do. You fooled me, you know.'

'In what way?'

'I assumed the Porsche was yours.'

Jack's teasing smile lit a fire in his eyes. 'I should've guessed you only wanted me for my car.' He slid his hands around her waist and leaned close enough to whisper in her ear. 'If it helps, I've got a brand-new, gleaming black Maserati back in Nashville.'

And that helps me how? The reality

of their vastly differing lifestyles slammed back into Gemma and she pulled away from him, struggling to ignore the confusion written all over his handsome face. 'I told April when she was trying to match-make the other day that I wasn't Cinderella and you certainly weren't Prince Charming come to whisk me away from all this.'

'Is this your way of telling me there's no hope for us?' Jack's blunt comment startled her, but she couldn't let him distract her from what she should've done the minute he came back into her life. 'Feel this.' He seized one of her hands and placed it right on top of his heart, the rapid thumping beat echoing through his shirt. 'It doesn't care about fancy cars and bank accounts. That's all irrelevant.'

A wave of sadness swept through her. 'Only a man who doesn't have to fret every month over how to pay the electric bill or where the next mortgage payment will come from could make such a careless statement. Love can't survive on fresh air. That's a fallacy created by rich people and romance novelists.'

His face turned to stone and Gemma briefly wished her words unsaid, but one of them had to face the truth and she seemed to have been allotted the thankless task.

'Will you at least allow me to drive you home?' Jack's quiet voice held nothing of his usual self-assurance. 'I don't want you waiting for a bus in the dark.' He held up his hands. 'I promise not to hassle you on the way. I won't even speak unless you ask me to.'

Gemma managed a brief nod. Very gently he rested his hand on her cheek, and she was sure she'd feel the imprint of his warm fingers in her dreams tonight.

In silence they made their way over to his parked car. If things had been different, she'd joke about the utilitarian vehicle, but nothing was funny anymore. She had an awful feeling it'd be a long time before she laughed again.

15

Sweat poured down Jack's face but he continued to haul junk out of the attic. Balancing a heavy box, he dragged it down the wobbly metal stairs and set it down on the floor. The men coming to install the roof insulation needed the space cleared out; and although Paul would've happily paid for someone else to do the work, Jack needed to physically exhaust himself. It was the only way to push away the memories of last night when Gemma's rejection sliced him to ribbons.

'Good grief. What *are* you doing?' Hannah Petersen's crisp voice cut through his self-absorption. He glanced down over the banister to see her standing in the middle of the entrance hall, laughing up at him. 'Do you mind if I come up?' She didn't wait for answer but bounded up the stairs to join him.

'Was I supposed to be expecting you?' Not really polite, but exactly how Jack felt at the moment.

She raised a perfectly shaped eyebrow and wagged her finger at him. 'Who's rattled your cage? I'm guessing it's a woman. It usually is.'

'Aren't you the smart one.'

Her sapphire-blue eyes danced with amusement. 'Gosh, she's really done a number on you.' Hannah's gaze ran down over him. 'Let's try again. Why don't you go and clean up and I'll take you out to lunch?'

Jack had a million and one things to do but remembered his manners and his job, both of which he preferred to hang on to. When he'd spoken to Paul yesterday his boss confirmed that he'd chosen Unique Restorations to work on West Dean House, and Hannah was to be in charge of the project. He'd found her vision for the house the most compatible with his own. Jack needed to backpedal and convince Hannah he wasn't a complete boor.

'I want to discuss the timetable and put a more detailed budget together,' she explained.

'Fine. If you'll excuse me, I'll go and shower.'

'Any problem if I take a look at this lot?' Hannah pointed to the trunks and boxes he had strewn around.

'Help yourself. Oh, and remind me to tell you about Mrs. Green's mother.'

'She sounds like the victim in an Agatha Christie mystery.' Hannah's smile was infectious and lightened Jack's grim mood. 'Hurry up. I'm starving.'

'You always are,' he retorted, and stalked off before she could come back with another smart remark.

Ten minutes later as he towelled himself dry, Jack realised he hadn't thought about Gemma for at least the last quarter of an hour. Was he so shallow that another woman's amusing conversation could distract him so easily? The idea bothered him, and he decided to be in strictly business mode when he returned to Hannah. He tugged on a clean pair of dark jeans and a blue and grey striped shirt. The blue sweater he usually wore as well was back in Nashville, so he grabbed his black leather jacket and slipped it on instead. Then he ran a comb through his damp hair and hurried back down the long corridor to the main entrance.

'Ah, a distinct improvement.' Hannah's eyes twinkled with mischief.

Jack's only response was a grunt as he gestured towards the door. 'I've got to be back by two for the roofers.'

'There's certainly no danger of you falling over yourself to impress your new contractor, is there?'

'I wasn't aware I needed to. You've already got the job. We'll work together fine, I'm sure.'

Hannah didn't say another word but gave him an enigmatic smile and glided past him to step outside. Jack suspected he was being set up but couldn't work out how or why. It'd give him something else to worry about, as if he didn't have enough already.

* * *

The shop door bell rang and Gemma started, not sure if she was disappointed or relieved to see April wander in. She'd had three customers today; two were only looking for directions and one bought an inexpensive scarf. None of them was Jack. It seemed he'd finally taken her at her word and was staying away.

'Rushed off your feet?' April joked, coming over to give her a hug. 'Harry's settled in front of the telly watching a new Batman DVD. I just popped out to see how Mum's getting on and pick up some fish for our tea. Would you like me to get you some too?'

Eating was the last thing on Gemma's mind. The joke Jack had made yesterday about her eating habits sneaked back into her brain and she blinked back tears.

'You don't have to get upset over a piece of cod.'

Gemma forced out a smile. 'Sorry. I've got a lot on my mind.'

April studied her intently. 'What happened with Lover Boy last night? I'm not sensing joy overflowing from you today.'

'It's a long story.' Gemma sighed. 'Let's just say there's not going to be a happy ending to the fairytale. Sorry, Fairy Godmother.'

'Is it anything to do with the cute blond I saw hanging on to Jack's every word in the Green Dragon just now?'

A pit opened in the base of Gemma's stomach and she thought she might be sick. 'Why were you in there?'

'Harry fancied a pasty for his lunch so I popped in and bought us a couple.' April glanced at her watch. 'I'd better not be long. I promised to get back to him before they went cold.'

An unwanted flash of jealousy sliced through Gemma. In a few short days Harry and April seemed to have eased from friendship into something deeper without a whole lot of aggravation. *He was beaten up trying to protect her. How much more aggravation would you like them to have?*

'So you and Jack are, um . . . '

'There *is* no me and Jack,' Gemma snapped. 'I made it clear last night that we don't have anything in common anymore. If he's moved on already, good for him.'

April's disbelief showed on her face but she didn't say a word.

'Off you go. Give Harry my love and tell him to rest. I really appreciate you looking out for him. I couldn't afford to close another day even if I've only sold enough to keep the lights on for another ten minutes.'

'My motives aren't entirely pure, you know,' April joked. 'I enjoyed telling Mother I was taking a day off, and spending time with Harry certainly won't be a hardship.' The colour deepened in her cheeks and she glanced down at the floor. 'I must be going.'

'You do that.' Gemma shooed her away and was left alone in an empty shop to think about Jack and his mystery blond. Had she panicked last night and found excuses to send him away because she was too scared to take another chance on him? Probably, she decided.

Trailing into the storeroom at the back of the shop, she turned on the kettle to make a cup of tea. She opened the biscuit tin because the situation called for at least one chocolate digestive, possibly two. She groaned aloud as a handful of boring Rich Tea biscuits stared back at her. The emergency stash of chocolate she kept in the small fridge was empty too, because she'd raided it on another dire day. Grouchier than ever, she made her tea and slammed the lid back on the biscuit tin.

She wandered back out to the shop and almost spilled her tea all over her at the sight of Jack standing outside on the pavement. He was more handsome than ever today in the black leather jacket she loved and a pair of tight-fitting jeans. He was talking intently to the most stunning woman she'd ever seen outside of a magazine. As he spoke he touched his companion's arm for emphasis, and the blond gazed up at him, drinking in every word. Gemma tried to rationalise what she was seeing. Jack was a tactile man; he'd told her once that it must be his Italian mother's genes, because it definitely didn't come from his English army officer father who wouldn't know an emotion if it stared him in the face. At seventeen she hadn't asked too much about his parents, but now it made her wonder. She stared back out the window to see them still engrossed in conversation.

He's always that way. Whoever he's with gets his full attention.

It was one of the reasons she loved him. Then she mentally smacked herself — she needed to stop this obsession with Jack for her own sanity. Turning her back to the window, she dug out a duster from under the counter and began to take ornaments off the nearest shelf to clean. With any luck, by the time she finished, Romeo and Juliet would have disappeared.

★   ★   ★

Out of the corner of his eye Jack registered how rigidly Gemma held herself. Her shoulders would kill her if she stayed in that position for long. After lunch they'd had enough time for him to give in to Hannah's plea that he introduce her to Mavis Green. The chance Gemma might spot them together was a bonus. After staying awake all night alternately furious and sad at Gemma for tossing away their chance for happiness as if it meant nothing, he'd come to a very scary conclusion. He loved her and was pretty sure she loved him back. So he intended to do whatever it took to change her mind about him. Maybe this wasn't the most subtle way, but if inciting her jealousy got his foot back in the door he'd go along with it.

'Do you mind if I come back to the house with you and work on some plans while you deal with the insulation people?' Hannah asked him.

Jack started as she prodded his arm. 'Sorry, did you say something?' With an indulgent smile she repeated herself. 'Oh yeah, of course. Not a problem.'

'Is that her?' She nodded towards Gemma's shop.

'Who?'

'The woman who's got you in knots.' She stared in the window. 'Pretty girl. Nice hair. Natural red, I'd say.'

Talking about his private life with work colleagues was against Jack's philosophy, but if he didn't tell someone he'd go mad. Hannah's easy manner and the sparkling engagement ring back on her finger today made it a no-brainer. 'On the way back I'd appreciate you giving me your opinion,' he said.

Hannah broke into a deep, throaty laugh. It'd surprised him the first time he heard it because it was completely at odds with her elegant, model-like appearance. 'You might regret saying that. I'll consider you've given me free rein to be totally honest. My mother says I have no filter and should learn to be more ladylike.'

Jack couldn't help laughing along with her. 'That's fine by me. I've been around straight-talking Americans for a decade and find I have to be cautious when I come back here so I don't give the impression of being rude.'

'Obviously you don't always succeed,' she teased.

Another smile tugged at his mouth and he gave in to it with a shrug. He unlocked the Range Rover and they both got in. Jack quickly drove off, and before he could change his mind he launched into the whole convoluted story of his relationship with Gemma. He purposely didn't look at Hannah, and occasionally she'd ask him a brief question, but most of the time she simply listened.

When they pulled up in front of the house, Jack wasn't in a hurry to get out. 'So what's the verdict?' he asked.

'You're an idiot.'

'Don't sugar-coat it, please.' Jack's sarcasm only made her smile.

'I completely understand why she's scared. Her life is precarious enough without throwing you into the mix. She's a proud woman who doesn't want to be seen as a gold-digger. You've got to prove yourself, and it won't be easy.' Hannah smirked. 'Of course, that part you'll have to work out yourself. I'm done with the free therapy.' She flung open the door and jumped out. 'Come on, we've got work to do. You can brood over the lovely Gemma later.'

Jack yearned to pull her back and make her spell out exactly what she thought he should do, but guessed he'd pushed his luck far enough for one day. He walked around to join her, and as they headed towards the house the sound of a car crunching on the rough gravel made him turn back around.

The black car stopped on the gravel and his father climbed out, stern-faced and unsmiling. Jack's heart thumped against the wall of his chest and he couldn't make himself speak.

16

'What on earth do *you* want with a place this size?' Philip ran his scathing gaze over the house and shook his head in disgust.

Jack struggled to get his brain working again. Surely if something had happened to his mother, even Philip wouldn't stand there making disparaging comments about a house. 'I'm overseeing the restoration for a client,' he explained.

'Paul Von Doorsten, I suppose.'

Jack didn't reply, but simply stared his father down.

'Fine. Don't say. It's nothing to me.'

Rather like me. Jack waited to be told why he was being honoured with this unexpected visit. There had to be a very good reason, and by his father's stiff demeanour he guessed it wasn't voluntary.

'We'd better go inside. I don't intend discussing personal family business out here.' Philip glanced across at Hannah, standing on the doorstep and flagrantly listening.

Jack stifled a smile. 'Certainly, sir,' he murmured, stepping to one side and letting his father walk in ahead. Hannah had suddenly disappeared and he guessed she'd have questions for him later. 'We can go to my rooms. I'll fix us some coffee.'

Philip's jaw worked hard and the furrows in his brow deepened. Jack waited for a refusal and was taken by surprise when his father nodded.

Silently they made their way down the long corridor. Jack considered telling him the history of the house and giving an overview of the restoration plans, but held his tongue. He opened the door and led the way into the rooms he'd appropriated for his own use. One was his bedroom with a very basic bathroom and the other he'd turned into a combination sitting room and impromptu kitchen. Jack put the kettle on to boil and dug out a jar of instant coffee from his sparse store cupboard.

'Do you still take yours black?' he asked his father. Philip told him once, in one of his rare moments of opening up, that his natural preference for cream and sugar in his coffee was knocked out of him in basic training. Anything other than black coffee was considered girly, but for some reason it was acceptable to drink milky, sweetened tea.

Philip nodded. 'I'm too old to change now.' His stern gaze rested on Jack as though he was trying to tell his only son something important without having to put it into words. At a wild guess Jack would say they weren't talking about coffee anymore.

He joined his father on the dilapidated red sofa he'd dragged down from the old servants' quarters at the top of the house and set their mugs down on the table. 'How's Mum?'

'She's about the same.' Philip's voice

cracked and he covered it up with a loud cough. 'Physically there's not much improvement, but the doctor's concerned about her . . . mental state.' His father never spoke about his feelings or emotions, considering it unmanly and un-British, and had a dim view of the medical profession.

'Is there anything I can do to help?'

Philip shrugged. 'She says if she could see you more and if, um, we could . . . get on better, it would ease her mind.' He planted his large hands on his thighs and Jack sensed the turmoil in his father's head.

'Does the doctor agree?'

'Of course,' he snorted. 'You know what those quacks are like. Anything to get them out of being responsible. I asked why he couldn't give her a few pills to sort it out but he said that wasn't a viable solution.'

Jack knew his father's old-fashioned opinion regarding prescription drugs and guessed he must've been desperate to make that suggestion. He supposed anything was better than being forced to see the son he detested and pretend to play some version of 'happy families' to please his wife. Once he asked his mother how she'd come to marry Philip and she'd patted his hand and smiled.

'I was at university in London studying English,' she'd told him, 'and my boyfriend at the time invited me to accompany him to his brother's army regimental dinner. Your father was seated across from me at the supper table and flirted with me all the way through the meal. He was so handsome and dashing in his uniform, and immediately whisked me off to dance as soon as the music started. My boyfriend never got a look in. And that was it.'

Jack had never been able to rationalise his mother's romantic memories with the stern, unyielding man who'd made his own childhood a misery.

'Come to tea again on Sunday,' Philip said.

Until the other day, Jack had neatly

stowed his parents in a mental box and sealed it up for his own sanity; but seeing his mother looking so fragile had shaken him. He couldn't turn his back on her again.

'Bring your girlfriend if you want.' The gruff instruction amused Jack, especially when he realised his father was talking about Hannah.

'Thanks, but the woman you saw earlier is Hannah Petersen, who's working with me on the house. We're not personally involved.'

For a second Philip's dark eyes held a gleam of humour. 'Pity.' It was the first time Jack had known his father to make something resembling a joke and he wasn't sure how to respond. 'I need to get back to your mother. I'll tell her to expect you at the weekend?'

'Of course.' How could he refuse?

Philip sprang up and smoothed down the creases in his trouser legs. 'There's no need for you to come out.'

'I'm expecting some contractors soon so I've got to make a move anyway.'

Jack glanced at his watch. 'They'll be here in a few minutes. I'll walk out with you.' He needed to gain back some of the momentum and establish the fact he wasn't a boy to be ordered around anymore.

Back outside they formally shook hands, and Jack stood almost at attention when his father got back in his car and drove off. He shoved his hands in his pockets and remembered Paul's words before he came here: 'I've got an interesting job for you, Jack. A few months in the mother country should put the spring back in your step. The ladies will fall over you and love your accent. Go enjoy yourself.'

Paul knew he was mixed up. So did Gemma, April and Hannah. Jack wondered why he'd been the last to realise it.

★   ★   ★

'Gem, April suggested I apply to do a graphic design course at Truro College.

What do you think?'

She put down the newspaper and glanced over at Harry. For someone who'd been through so much in the last forty-eight hours, he sounded remarkably cheerful. She hated to burst his bubble, but it was ingrained in her to be the practical, responsible one. 'I'm sure you'd be good at it . . . ' she began.

'But?'

' . . . but you and I both know your attention span is limited and you find it hard to concentrate for long. April hasn't been around you as much; she might not realise.' A deeply etched frown marred Harry's smile. Maybe she should wish the words unspoken, but one of them needed to be realistic.

'If I don't try I'll never know, will I? She says these days they're used to dealing with students with ADHD and similar disorders and would help me.'

Gemma heard the echo of her friend's upbeat voice in his reply and knew she'd have to give in gracefully and simply hope he didn't get hurt.

Harry moved over to sit by her and held her hand.

'You've been here for me when no one else was,' he said, 'and I'm not ever going to forget that. April's never going to replace you in here, Gem.' He pressed her hand against his heartbeat and a rush of tears pricked her eyes. 'But I want more out of life now. I've been safe too long.' A nod was all she could manage and luckily it did the trick, so his smile returned. 'It wouldn't be right away, because I've got to start painting again and get a portfolio of work together. If it goes well I'll apply, and if not I'll come up with something else.'

Harry's positive attitude infected her and in a flash she saw him through April's eyes — a handsome, funny, intelligent man with obstacles to overcome, like most people. Everyone had their problems; some were visible and others hidden from view. Hers was an acute case of over-responsibility mixed with a dissatisfaction in the direction of her life. Maybe Harry's epiphany would give her the shake-up she needed too.

The bright smile she plastered over her face was almost genuine. It'd take time to adjust to Harry's new version of his old life, but she was determined to get there sooner rather than later. 'That's a good plan,' she said.

'Thanks, Gem.' He rested his head on her shoulder and they sat there quietly.

'Oh.' Gemma started as the doorbell jangled, disturbing the peaceful moment. 'Who's that now? You aren't expecting April back, are you?'

'Unfortunately not,' Harry teased, a wicked smile tugging at his mouth.

Gemma reluctantly got up. Halloween wasn't for another few days, so it'd better not be children begging for sweets. She unlocked the door and opened it enough to peek out. Her heart sunk when she saw Jack on the step. 'What are you doing here?'

'I came to see how Harry was doing.'

'You could've rung and asked.'

He took a step closer and Gemma caught a hint of his warm, spicy aftershave. 'Then I wouldn't have seen you, would I?' His low, tantalising drawl teased her exactly as he'd surely intended.

'Who is it?' Harry yelled. Very reluctantly she answered, knowing what her brother would say next. 'Great. Tell him to come in.'

Gemma sighed and stood back out of the way to let Jack slide past her.

'Thanks.'

'Don't thank me,' she groused. 'I'd have given you an update on Harry and sent you on your way.'

'Really?' Jack's bright green eyes pinned her down. 'Don't lie, Gemma. We're too old for all that.'

'Are we?' she croaked.

'We sure are.' He reached over and tweaked her nose. 'You simply haven't realised it yet.' He slung his arm around her shoulder and half-pushed, half-walked her into the living room. 'How's it going, Harry?'

'I'll leave you to talk and make some coffee.' Gemma escaped to the kitchen, collapsing against the counter while she took several slow, deep breaths in an effort to control the wild emotions coursing through her. When she was seventeen Jack had tied her in knots every time he got close, and things were no different twenty years later. *Don't lie, Gemma. We're too old for all that.* Was he right? If he was, where did that leave her?

17

'Harry, do me a favour,' Jack whispered and scooted over closer to his friend's armchair. Gemma was out of sight and hopefully hearing.

'What do you need?'

'You out of the way,' he murmured. 'No offence, but I really need to talk to your sister alone, and she's being a bit . . . '

'Stroppy?'

'Yep.' Jack strove to be honest. 'For good reasons.'

'So you need to grovel?'

'Got it in one.'

'I'll tell her I'm tired and take my coffee upstairs.' Harry's conspiratorial grin had Jack stifling the laughter threatening to erupt from his throat. 'She'll believe me because I've never given her any reason not to.' He chuckled. 'Not since I was a teenager, anyway.'

Gemma walked in carrying a tray and stared suspiciously at them both. 'What're you two up to?'

'Harry was telling me about the design course he's hoping to do,' Jack said. That wasn't a lie, just not the complete truth.

'Right. Why do I not believe you?'

'Can't imagine. Can you, Harry?' Jack asked, needing back-up, and Harry dutifully obliged, jumping up from the chair and going into his tired, headachy spiel. Jack almost felt guilty when Gemma instantly went into worried, responsible-sister mode. She'd been through a lot the last few days and now Jack had unintentionally added to her stress. But he told himself it was necessary to break eggs to make a decent omelette, and kept his mouth shut.

Finally they were alone, but his hope that she'd join him on the sofa faded as she stood well out of reach and glared hard enough to frighten off most men. Thank goodness he wasn't most men.

'Satisfied?' she said.

He considered pretending he didn't have a clue what she was talking about, but with honesty on the menu for tonight it'd be a huge mistake on his part. 'Yeah, I am. Do you *really* mind?' His words acted like a pinprick on a balloon and he watched Gemma's anger drain away. He patted the space next to him on the sofa and waited, his racing heartbeat so loud he was sure she must hear it.

Gemma set the tray on the table and quietly sat down. He dared to rest his hand on her knee and she leaned against his shoulder, neither of them saying a word. He tried to decide how best to apologise, but before he could speak she beat him to it.

'I was a fool at the hospital.' Her hushed voice cracked and he watched her struggle to keep going. 'Do you know what made me see sense?'

Jack hoped it was the sight of him but suspected there was more to her revelation. When she glanced at him her soft, grey eyes were swimming with tears. 'It was seeing April and Harry together. They have such faith in each other and truly believe they can overcome any obstacles as long as they're together. And they nearly missed out — mainly because I'd forced Harry into a safe, narrow existence in my version of protecting him.'

Jack pushed back an auburn curl from her face, noticing a few threads of grey running through her hair. The reminder that she wasn't the teenager he'd fallen in love with all those years ago sobered him. 'Never blame yourself for taking care of him the best way you knew how. He wouldn't have survived without you.'

She shrugged. 'I suppose so, but please let me beat myself up a little. I enjoy being a martyr sometimes.' A touch of humour crept back into her voice.

'Fair enough,' Jack teased. 'Although I might call you Gemma of Arc if you do it too often.' He wasn't sure how to phrase his next question, but yet again she beat him to it.

'Don't ask me how I think this is going to work out, or even if it will in the long run, but I want to give it — us — a chance,' Gemma blurted out, blushing so hard Jack felt the heat rising from her skin. 'They always say you shouldn't regret the things you have done, because they're all experience. Only regret the things you haven't done.'

He pressed a soft kiss on her mouth. 'I won't ever regret you.'

'What were you about to say just now?' Gemma asked. A fraction of the shine left his eyes and for a moment she was afraid.

'I wanted to try to explain how I feel about you and the rest of my life, but it's hard.' The rasp had returned to his voice.

'Small steps. Tell me one thing for now and leave the rest for another day.'

Hesitantly he began to talk, and

within a few minutes he'd broken her heart. The mental picture of a small boy longing for nothing more than his father's love and approval, but never getting it, tore at Gemma.

'I want to feel sorry for him, but I'm not sure I can.' Jack sat up straighter and clutched her shoulders. 'Thanks.'

'What for?'

'Understanding. I never talk about him because it brings up too many bad memories. The only way I've been able to move forward at all is to ignore it as far as possible.' He shook his head. 'But that's not working anymore.' Then he hurried to explain about his mother. 'I made a big mistake staying away all these years.'

'You did it for a good reason.' Gemma managed a tiny smile. 'Your reasoning was flawed but you meant well, in your typical bumbling male way.'

'I appreciate your efforts to make me feel better.' The touch of irony was far more like the Jack she knew and loved.

'Maybe your mum getting ill will turn out to be a blessing in disguise.'

He stared at her in disbelief. 'On what planet could you possibly think that?'

'Would you have gone to visit if she was well? Would you have listened to your father when he came yesterday?'

Jack flinched and shook his head. The merest hint of a smile curved the edges of his mouth and he sighed. 'Of course you're right. You would be. Women keep telling me things I don't want to hear. You. April. My mother, and . . . '

'And who?'

'Nothing. My tongue's trying to catch up with my mind.'

You're lying to me, Jack Watson, but I'll let you get away with it simply because you've been through enough for now. Gemma was determined not to ask him about the mystery blond. Until he proved otherwise, she decided to trust him.

'Are you busy on Sunday afternoon?' he asked her.

She'd hoped to get a few more hours of work in the pub but kept that to herself. Jack needed her. *More than the electricity bill needs to be paid?* Pushing the thought away, she shook her head.

'Would you come to Plymouth with me?'

'Of course.'

He dropped light, teasing kisses all over her face and his grin melted her resolve all over again. 'You're an angel. I could rent the pretty car again.'

'There's no need.' Gemma gave a rueful smile. 'My big mouth got me in enough trouble over that car.' Jack played with her hair, and she sensed him hesitate, guessing he wasn't sure how to respond. 'I'm not pretending I'm okay with the whole money issue. We never had much growing up, but we had what we needed and it was enough. I've struggled to take care of Harry and keep the business going without any-one's help.'

'And you'd hate anyone to think you

were after me for my money. Right?' He'd hit the nail on the head and a giant lump formed in her throat. 'Remember that we know better, and we're the only two people who matter in all this.' He wrapped his arms around her and his solid warmth made everything right again. 'Are you good now?'

She nodded and felt him smile.

'I'd better go. We've both got work to get up for in the morning.'

'How's the house coming on?' Gemma asked.

'Good. Would you like to come over and see inside?'

She'd heard that the locals contracted to work on West Dean House weren't allowed to talk about the project, and very little had slipped out about what exactly was being done. The fact that Jack trusted her meant a lot. 'I'd love to,' she said.

'How about I pick you up on Sunday, and we'll have a picnic lunch at the house before I show you around? Then we'll go to visit my folks,' Jack suggested. 'Or do you have to be here to cook for Harry?'

'I'm sure April will be happy to help out.' She laughed. 'Maybe she'll take him to her mother's for lunch. That'll throw the cat among the pigeons.'

'Mrs. Broad isn't a fan of Harry, I assume?'

'Hardly.' Gemma snorted. 'I don't know what she's said to April about this new development between them, but I'm sure she'll be dead set against it.'

'It's so easy for parents to negatively affect their children's lives without realising it,' Jack murmured, and she knew they weren't talking about Harry anymore. 'You were lucky. I used to envy you so much.' He cleared his throat and ploughed on. 'My family had money, and I went to the best schools, but every time I came into this house I knew you were the wealthy one.'

Gemma blinked back tears as Jack struggled to explain how the obvious love in her family made him feel.

'I don't mind admitting I was jealous,' he said with a resigned shrug. 'But the good side was that it showed me things didn't have to be the way they were at my house.'

'Is that why you've never married?' His eyes darkened and she was afraid she'd been too forward. 'You don't have to answer.'

'Yeah, I do, but if I'm too honest it might freak you out.' He flashed a wry grin. 'My family situation is a large part of my reluctance, but also . . . I never met anyone to match you.'

Now Gemma really was stunned. Of course it was the same for her, minus the unhappy home situation, but he was the one who'd been brave enough to say it aloud.

Jack picked up her hands and smiled. 'You're shaking. I didn't mean to scare you, and I don't expect you to — '

She kissed him, silencing his rambling. Then she told him, 'Harry isn't the only reason I never went out with anyone seriously after you, either.' Her stomach churned and she almost lost her nerve. 'All the other men were never you.'

Jack lifted up their hands and planted tiny, feathered kisses on her fingers. 'That's all I need for now,' he declared. 'There's a lot to work out, isn't there? We aren't kids. We've got complicated lives.' He leaned closer so their foreheads touched. 'I won't be around much the next couple of days because I've got a lot of work going on, but I'll call.'

'We can do the teenage talking-on-the-phone-for-hours thing,' she joked.

'Works for me,' he said, going along with her attempt to lighten the conversation. 'Come on, kid, Prince Charming needs to return to his castle and Cinderella ought to get her beauty sleep.' He grinned. 'Not that she needs it, of course.'

Gemma loved how he made her feel like a young girl in love for the first time. 'Of course not. Cinderella was well known for having dark circles under her eyes, the beginnings of wrinkles, and the distinct need to cover up a few grey hairs.'

Suddenly Jack's expression changed, going from laughing to serious in the blink of an eye. 'You've always been beautiful to me and always will be. What's here is gorgeous.' He stroked his fingers lightly down her face. 'But the generous, loving nature nestled in here is what really matters.' He placed his right hand over her rapidly beating heart.

'Go, before I say something it's too soon for,' she pleaded, loving the flash of acknowledgement in his mesmerising green eyes.

He nodded and stood up without another word. Reluctantly they walked out to the hall together and lingered for a few more minutes on the doorstep. When they finally said goodnight, Gemma watched him leave and knew they were in this together again. She wondered if there was a chance they'd get their happy ending at last, but hardly dared to hope.

18

The loud rumble of sanding machines smoothing out the old wood floors and workmen shouting from one end of the house to the other had given Jack a thumping headache. He threw on his heavy wool coat and made a strategic retreat outside. The stiff easterly wind stung his face as soon as he stepped out of the front door but he strode off down the driveway at a brisk pace. He'd promised Paul that the worst of the potholes and overgrown trees would be dealt with, so he'd check that out now and make notes on what needed to be done.

'Wait for me!' Hannah shouted, and he turned around to see her running towards him. He put on a polite smile and did as she asked, cursing the fact that he hadn't slipped out quietly enough. He wasn't in the mood for company. Gemma had sounded distracted on the phone last night and he sensed that she was going over and over again in her head everything they'd talked about. A sensible woman at heart, she'd likely managed to talk herself out of taking a chance alongside of him. He wished he had the time to go and see her before Sunday, but he was on a tight schedule and couldn't afford to slack off.

'Can I talk to you about making a few changes to the plans while you walk?' Hannah asked him.

He explained what he'd been about to do and hoped she'd get the hint that this wasn't a good time.

'Perfect. I could do with a walk. I'll shut up until we reach the gate at the other end and then talk your ear off on the way back,' she declared with a bright smile.

I can hardly wait. 'Fine.' He left it at that and set off walking again. The recent heavy rains had deepened the already dangerous potholes, but they'd be fairly easy to fix. Cutting back the overgrown vegetation would mean more hard labour but Paul had no set budget, wanting nothing but the best for his bride-to-be. Jack's orders were to get as much done in as short a time as possible. Obviously he wasn't to waste money, but his boss wouldn't expect him to skimp either.

'Those will have to be replaced.' Hannah pointed to the dilapidated wooden gates, tied back out of the way for the moment. 'I've got a lot of contacts around Cornwall. If you'd like, I could put out some feelers to my various sources to find you some suitable gates.'

'That would be helpful. Thanks.'

She glanced at her watch. 'Drat. I forgot I've got an important call to make. We'll have a chat later.' Before Jack could respond, she took off sprinting and soon disappeared out of sight. He scribbled down a few more ideas in his notebook while they were fresh in his head and then set off back towards the house.

He kicked off his muddy boots inside the door and padded down the corridor in his stocking feet to get some clean shoes to wear. As he passed by the library he noticed the door was half-open and reached out to close it. He preferred to keep the areas they weren't working on shut up as far as possible. As he reached for the door knob he heard Hannah's low voice drifting out from inside. He would've gone off and left her alone but froze when she suddenly mentioned Thea's name.

'Don't worry. No one's guessed my connection with the great Thea Barrington. I'm not stupid. I've got my work cut out, but trust me, I can get around Jack Watson. He's a pussycat. Lowering my price to get the contract was galling, but I know you'll make it up to me.' Hannah laughed and lowered her voice so Jack couldn't catch what she said next. He'd heard enough. The woman was playing him for a fool but he didn't know why.

Jack hurried away so she wouldn't catch him eavesdropping. He needed time to think. If this surprise blew up in Paul's face, Jack would be out of a job. *Pussycat.* He'd give her pussycat.

★ ★ ★

Harry mushed his cornflakes down into the milk but made no effort to eat.

'What's up with you?' Gemma asked him. 'I thought you were looking forward to working with Pippa the rest of the week.' Pippa, a friend of Gemma's, wanted to revamp her small art shop in the village and had hired Harry to help her. 'You're not going to let her down, are you?'

'Of course not,' he grouched. 'I'm worried about April.'

Gemma was cautious of making any sort of joke; the relationship was too new for that.

Harry's slate-grey eyes darkened and Gemma tried not to show her panic.

She'd seen him this way many times before, although not for several years now, and it wasn't good. Frustrated by emotions he couldn't control, they'd build up in him until he snapped. Sometimes he'd hide out in his room and refuse to eat or talk to her for days. Then he'd emerge as if nothing had happened and they'd carry on as usual.

'Loosen up, Gem. I'm all right, just angry, like a normal person. Okay?'

She nodded but surreptitiously crossed her fingers under the table.

'Mrs. Broad is being nasty to April. She made her cry last night.' He managed a tight smile. 'April, I mean. Not the old dear.'

'Did they argue about you?' Gemma spelt it out; there wasn't much point in doing otherwise.

'Mainly.' He dropped the spoon in the soggy cereal and pushed the bowl away. 'No one would be good enough for April, but especially not a lazy, useless man like me — apparently.' His wry smile couldn't cover the hurt laced through his voice. 'Mrs. Broad doesn't want April to have a life outside of the shop and their home. She likes having April at her beck and call. I'm spoiling that for her.'

Gemma gave his hand a comforting squeeze. 'I'm glad you can see it's not simply you.'

'The main part of it is, though. And who's to say she's not right?' This was what Gemma had tried to protect him from all these years — other people's ignorance. 'I'm not much of a prospect, am I?' His words pinned her down and she didn't have a clue how to reply without hurting him even more.

'Is it silly to ask if you're serious about April?'

The merest hint of a smile returned to his face. 'Yes, very silly, Gem.' He took a swallow of his tea and stared off into the distance. 'No steady job. Very little money in the bank. Can't drive.'

Gemma flinched. Hearing his drawbacks laid out so plainly was heartbreaking.

'I don't have much to offer April, do I?'

Jack's words made her think: 'April's a sensible woman and anyone can see she loves him. It's not a bad start. Harry's a decent man. He deserves this.' In her own quiet way she'd defended Harry for years. Now he needed her to do it more openly. If she didn't stand up for him, who would?

'You have a lot to offer, Harry. You're a decent man with a kind heart. April turned down Jimmy Steadman's proposal years ago because he was a sour-faced, bad-tempered man who covered it up well. Mrs. Broad wasn't happy with her then because he was rolling in money and came from a 'good' family. But April told me at the time she'd rather die a spinster than marry him.' Gemma hesitated because she wasn't sure if she should tell Harry any more. It wasn't fair to hold out on him. 'At the time I asked her if she still held a candle for you.'

'What did she say?' Harry whispered,

grabbing her hand.

'She had tears in her eyes and said she'd always love you, but that we must never talk about it again because it hurt too much that you couldn't remember.' A tear trickled down her cheek and Harry gently brushed it away. 'We never did.'

'Until the other day?'

She inclined her head and couldn't speak.

'I'm glad you did. Very glad.' His fervent words lifted her heart and she met his eyes, now a sparkling bright silver and brimming over with love.

'So am I.' Gemma touched Harry's arm. 'It's going to work out. You have to be patient. This isn't easy for April either.'

'Thanks, Gem. You're the best.' He pushed the chair back and jumped up, taking his dirty dishes over to the sink. 'Are you and Jack, um, a couple again?'

'I think so.'

'That's a bit vague,' he chided.

She sighed. 'It's complicated. We're working on it.'

'We're a sad pair,' Harry declared. He put the plug in the sink and turned on the hot tap, then picked up the tea towel and tossed it over to her. 'I'll wash. You wipe.'

Thankful he didn't ask any more questions, Gemma started to dry the dishes. She had enough confusion running around her brain without trying to explain something she didn't understand herself yet.

★ ★ ★

Jack finished giving instructions to the electrician. Hannah was hovering behind him but he chose not to acknowledge her yet. He sent the man off to start work, then turned and pretended to be surprised. 'Hannah. I didn't realise you were there. What can I do for you?'

'Do you have time now to discuss a few ideas I've got?'

He checked his watch and frowned. 'I can give you about thirty minutes.'

'Okay.' She dragged out the word and gave him a curious look. 'Is everything all right?'

Yeah. I love being tricked. It's my favourite thing. He tossed the question right back at her: 'Any reason why it shouldn't be?'

'Not that I know of,' she stammered. 'But you seem . . . upset.'

Jack plastered on a fake smile. He intended to reel her in soon but wanted to give her more line to tie herself up with first. 'Oh, no. I've a lot on my mind, that's all.' He rested his hand on her shoulder. 'How about we get some coffee and take it into the ballroom?'

'Are you going to sing for me again?' she teased.

'That was a one-off. I gave up music a long time ago.'

'I can't imagine why. You've got a great voice.'

The genuine compliment swept the rug out from under his feet and Jack steeled himself not to soften towards her. He hadn't been mistaken in what he'd overheard. 'You go on in and I'll bring our drinks,' he said. 'Milk and no sugar, right?'

She nodded, but he could tell by her diffidence that he'd set her on edge. He hurried off towards his rooms and tried to decide the best way to tackle the problem. Should he come right out with it, or be more subtle? In business he'd had a lot of practice in doing both, but the trick was knowing which to choose for maximum effect. He took his time fixing their coffees and set the mugs on a tray with a packet of biscuits before heading back to join her.

'Right, here we are,' he said heartily when he returned.

Hannah had made herself comfortable on an old sofa, once elegant but sorely in need of re-upholstering, in front of the large floor-to-ceiling windows looking out over the garden. Jack set the tray down on a small rickety Chinese inlaid table and hoped it wouldn't give way. He pulled up a chair to sit across from her, disliking the fact that he was about to destroy the budding friendship they'd slipped into; but he was here to do a job and his priority was to protect his boss's interests.

Jack fixed her with a hard stare, and two pink circles coloured her cheeks. 'Let's cut out the small talk,' he said. 'You're going to tell me who you were talking to about Thea Barrington and what you're really doing here.'

19

'It's not what you think.'

Hannah's quiet response, so unlike her usual self-assured manner, unsettled Jack, but he stayed resolute. 'And what might that be?'

'I'm not going to reveal to the world the reason why Paul Von Doorsten bought West Dean House, if that's what you're afraid of.' A touch of defiance sneaked back into her voice and Jack reluctantly admired her for not backing down.

'How would you know the answer to that question, anyway?' Jack persisted. His boss had been very careful discussing the renovations with all the possible contractors and had never gone into details about why he'd acquired the house.

Hannah couldn't quite meet his gaze and fiddled with the hem of her sleeve before picking up her coffee to take a sip. 'I can't tell you.'

He was tired of playing games. 'If you don't lay it out right now, I'll get on the phone to Paul and explain the situation. My advice will be for him to sue your company for breach of contract.' He leaned forward. 'Remember the clause that specified complete secrecy?' Hannah nodded. 'Unique Restorations' reputation will be trash by the time Paul finishes with you.'

Hannah slumped and covered her face with her hands. 'Fine. You win.' She straightened up and gave him a wry smile. 'I told Thea this wouldn't work.'

'Excuse me?' Jack couldn't make any sense of what she was saying. 'Were you speaking to Thea earlier?'

'Yes,' she conceded. 'I'm sorry for not being honest. I was only trying to do my big sister a favour.'

'Sister?' He must sound like a parrot. He shoved his hand through his hair, messing up any style it might've had. 'You and Thea Barrington are sisters?'

'Well, half-sisters, if we're splitting hairs. We have the same father but different mothers,' Hannah explained. Hurrying on, she launched into a long, complicated story about Thea's long-time obsession with English country houses. 'She discovered Paul had selected you to find him a suitable one to buy for a wedding present.'

'How?'

Her cheeks flamed. 'She's a woman, Jack. She checks his phone and reads his emails. It's what we do.'

He didn't comment, pretty sure Gemma would never stoop to such a thing. 'I still don't get where *you* come into all this.'

'Thea saw the instructions Paul gave you and panicked. She had visions of ending up with a tacky recreation of Downton Abbey, which she'd then have to pretend she liked.'

Everything clicked into place and he shook his head in amused disbelief. 'So Thea calls her interior decorator sister and cunningly makes sure you get the job. You could easily impress Paul by filtering his future wife's vision through your plans. Paul's a brilliant business-man, but he wouldn't know a Regency chair if he fell over it.' Jack chuckled.

'Are you still going to tell him?' Hannah frowned and reached over to touch his hand. 'Surely he doesn't need to know? This way he gets to 'surprise' her and she'll be happy.'

Jack hated dishonesty but could see her point. What would he achieve by revealing the deception to his boss? Nothing except upsetting the happy couple and possibly causing a rift between them. 'Is your connection with Thea commonly known?' he asked.

'No. My mother brought me back here to live after her marriage broke up. Very few people even know I have any family in America. Thea keeps her private life as quiet as she can too. She's never been one for a lot of Hollywood flash.'

Jack was forced to admit she was right. Thea's public appearances mainly occurred when she was promoting a new film. Paul, who was reserved to the point of almost being reclusive, would never have fallen in love with a woman who loved publicity for the sake of it.

'I suppose we might get away with it.'

Hannah's smile returned at his choice of the word 'we'. 'I'm sure Thea will be very grateful.'

Jack threw up his hands. 'Keep me out of it, please. You can let her think you pulled a fast one on me. All you need to do is your job, and I'll agree with everything you suggest.' He grinned. 'Apart from if you go crazy and want to rip the original fabric of the house apart and turn the place into a quasi-Victorian theme park.'

She burst into giggles, then laughed so hard tears ran down her face. 'Oh, Jack. You're impossible.'

'I try.' He'd hated the idea of Hannah being some kind of spy ready to splash the news about Paul and his secret romantic wedding present all over the place, and his relief was immense. 'Now we've got that out of the way, we'd better talk about what you really wanted discuss earlier.'

'I thought you were meeting some-one?'

'I lied.' Jack smiled. 'You're not the only devious one.'

'Obviously not.' Hannah opened up the folder she'd brought in and spread it out on the table. 'Right. Here's what the real boss wants.'

They both laughed and prepared to settle down to work, but before they could start Hannah's phone buzzed with a new text message. As she read it all the colour drained from her face and she swayed where she sat.

'What's wrong?' Jack asked.

She didn't answer, only stared at him with tear-glazed eyes.

★ ★ ★

Gemma struggled to look objectively at the shop. Her parents bought it back in the mid 1970s after her father left the

Royal Navy and it was supposed to be their retirement fund. Unfortunately it hadn't worked out that way. Instead they'd died together in a fiery car crash just outside London on their way to celebrate their silver wedding anniversary.

There were two main problems with the business: they'd never done enough to differentiate themselves from the other gift shops in Trewarne, and Gemma never had her parents' enthusiasm for the business. To her it was simply a way to make a living for herself and Harry — and these days it barely did that anymore.

She dare not let herself think too much about Jack, because if she did she'd get nowhere. Before she could consider a possible future for them together, she needed to make up her own mind about the direction she wanted her life to go in. The possibility that she might not have to consider Harry as much was a novel idea she hadn't got her head around yet.

Cornwall was in her heart and soul, but the lure of experiencing life elsewhere was tempting. Maybe this was her chance to do the things she'd yearned to do as a young girl. If Harry could consider going to college, why shouldn't she expand her own horizons?

Gemma had always loved history and planned to teach, fired up by the notion of inspiring students with her own love of the past. She was a great believer in the theory that it was necessary to understand the past to be able to move forward.

Now you're back to Jack again.

She sighed. Everything came back to him. As teenagers they'd shared their dreams for a future lived together. When he went back to London he'd promised to write every day, phone when he could, and come back to visit her as often as possible. After she finished school the following year the plan was for her to go to university while he started his singing career.

'My father's got other plans for me

228

but I'm not going to go along with them, Gem,' Jack had said. 'He wants me to join the army like he did, but he doesn't understand it's not for me.'

But there hadn't been a single letter or telephone call, and it'd broken her heart. Before she could pluck up the courage to ask his Aunt Marion if she'd heard anything from him, Gemma's mother had heard that the older woman was in hospital and not expected to recover. Marion's death a couple of months later ended any connection with Jack, and Gemma had been forced to go on without him.

She glanced at the clock with relief. It was time to lock up the shop, and thankfully April and Harry were going out, so she didn't have to rush home to cook.

Go and see Jack. That's what you really want to do.

He said he'd be busy.

But he won't mind if you stop by to say hello.

He might. I don't want to annoy him and be needy.

Would it be so terrible if he realises you need him?

The conversation ricocheted around her head until she came close to screaming. She was a thirty-seven-year-old woman, for goodness sake. If she couldn't pay a brief visit to the man she loved, there was something wrong.

She locked the door and flipped over the 'open' sign to 'closed', then made her way into the back of the shop and took a few minutes to freshen up. She shook her hair loose from the sensible ponytail it'd been tied up in all day and gave it a good brush. With a layer of pink lip gloss, a touch of blusher, and a quick spray of the light floral perfume Jack had commented on last week, she was as ready as she ever would be. The dark jeans and purple jumper she'd worn all day weren't glamorous, but Jack wouldn't expect her to be model-girl perfect. Thank heavens he seemed to love the natural look she'd never tried too hard to change. Gemma knew that as soon as she saw Jack, her worries would shift into perspective. He'd wrap his warm arms around her and make her feel special again.

Swinging her car keys, she hurried out of the back door and jumped into her old Ford Fiesta parked on the street. She hummed to herself as she drove out of the village and made her way along the coast, taking the narrow, winding road carefully in the fading light. Just in time she spotted the sign for West Dean House and jerked the wheel hard to pull in through the open gates. Her car bumped over numerous potholes as she crept down the driveway. Obviously they hadn't got to the top of Jack's to-do list yet.

She came to a stop by the front door and got out of the car. For a minute she stood and stared at the impressive house, remembering the last time she'd been there. It'd been when old Mr. Dean opened the grounds to the public for a fête to raise money for the village church. She must've been about fifteen at the time and recalled going with

April and a few of their friends.

She spotted Jack's Range Rover and then saw an elegant silver Mercedes parked by the side door. If Jack had an important visitor, he might not appreciate her stopping by.

Stop being a coward.

She smoothed down her hair and walked purposefully towards the front door. She tried ringing the rusty bell but guessed it wasn't working when she didn't hear anything. Next she lifted the heavy iron knocker in the shape of a pineapple and banged it a couple of times, but there was still no response. When she fiddled with the door it opened easily, so she stepped inside and called out Jack's name.

Large double doors on the other side of the expansive hall stood open on one side, and a noise came from inside the room that sounded almost like a woman crying. Gemma tiptoed across the tiled floor and peeped in. With his black hair gleaming under the light from the chandeliers, Jack stood in the middle of the room with his arms wrapped around a young woman. It was the same blond Gemma saw him talking to outside her shop, only now the woman was sobbing her heart out.

'Why, Jack? She's not even pretty. She's old and boring.'

Gemma slapped her hand across her mouth, certain she'd be ill if she stood there another minute. She didn't wait to hear Jack's reply but raced from the house, slamming the front door behind her. Her shaking hands couldn't work the key at first, but finally she managed to get into the car. She almost flooded the engine in her hurry to get it started, but it chugged into life and she roared off down the driveway. In the back of her mind she knew she ought to slow down but instead pushed the accelerator to the floor.

As the gates came into view, Gemma saw in her rear-view mirror that someone was flashing their bright lights at her. But she'd listened to the last of Jack's promises and wasn't about to stop. Suddenly she caught the edge of a pothole with her front right tyre, and a scream ripped from her throat as the car swerved off the road. She slammed on the brakes, but it was too late. The loud, jarring crunch of metal ripping apart filled her head and everything went black.

20

Jack leapt out of the car with his heart in his throat and raced to get to Gemma. Her door was badly dented where she'd hit the tree but he tugged on the handle until it wrenched free. 'Are you all right?' he pleaded, afraid to touch her in case she was hurt and he made it worse.

'I think so,' Gemma whispered and looked around at him, grimacing as she turned her neck. 'My poor car.'

Jack bit his tongue. He'd been about to say her car was on its last legs anyway, but she wouldn't appreciate his candour. 'I'm going to help you out.'

She brushed away his hand as he reached into the car. 'Leave me alone,' she yelled, her voice shaking with anger. 'I can manage.'

Jack stood back out of the way, feeling helpless as Gemma struggled to undo the seatbelt and then cautiously swung her legs out of the car. She pushed herself up to standing but instantly crumpled, and he leapt forward. He barely managed to catch her before she would've hit the ground, and swept her up into his arms.

'Whether you like it or not, I'm taking care of you,' he said. 'I'll put your obstinacy down to shock.' While he deposited her in the front passenger seat of his car, she said nothing and only turned to stare blankly out of the window. Very slowly, being careful to drive around the potholes, he made his way back to the house. 'Sit there and I'll get you out.' She didn't protest, but when he lifted her out she stiffened in his arms.

Hannah came rushing out to meet them. 'What on earth happened? Is there anything I can do?'

'She was driving too fast and hit a tree,' Jack explained. 'Luckily it wasn't head-on, but I'm pretty sure her car's totalled. I don't think she's seriously hurt, but I'm going to take her to the hospital to be checked out.'

'No you're not,' Gemma protested. 'I'm fine. I'll call someone to come and get me.'

Jack's puzzlement grew, but he suddenly caught her glaring at Hannah and things clicked into place. He'd bet anything she'd spotted him comforting the other woman, put two and two together, and made fifty million out of it. Did she really not trust him any more than that?

'We'll discuss this inside,' he stated in a tone of voice that he hoped made it clear she'd better not argue. 'Hannah, could you make a mug of strong, sweet tea for Gemma, please?'

'I don't — ' Gemma began.

'Yes, you do,' he insisted, and she sunk back into a moody silence as he carried her into the house.

'Of course.' Hannah smiled and hurried off.

'Very amenable, isn't she?' Gemma sniped, and if Jack hadn't been afraid of dropping her he'd have roared with laughter. He'd never seen her this jealous before.

'When I have you sitting down and you've calmed down some,' he said, 'I'll introduce you to Hannah.'

She snorted. 'I have no desire to meet your . . . whatever she is.'

'Work colleague. Her company is doing the interior decoration for the house and she's in charge of the project.'

'I'm sure she is.' Gemma managed to imbue the few words with deeply scathing criticism. Jack ignored her and carried her into the ballroom to set her gently down on the sofa, reaching for a couple of cushions and tucking them behind her back. Then he pulled a chair over closer and sat down.

'Before Hannah comes back in you're going to listen to me, Gemma.'

'What if I don't want to?'

He was getting exasperated now. 'Gemma, you know how much I love you. I've loved you for twenty years,

238

you silly girl. I thought you loved me too, but you obviously don't trust me or you wouldn't act this way.' It was hard to hide his sadness and he had to look away.

The sight of Jack, shaken and uncertain because of her foolishness, was too much after the shock of the crash. Large, hot tears streamed down Gemma's face and she tried in vain to brush them away. Jack came over to sit by her and gathered her into his arms, murmuring all the time how much he loved her. He rubbed his large hands tenderly over her back and told her it would be all right. At the moment she couldn't see how it ever would be, but was too worn out to argue. Quietly he began to tell her all about Hannah Petersen, and the more he explained the worse Gemma felt.

'It wasn't that I tried to hide her from you,' he said with a shrug. 'It just didn't seem relevant.' He hesitated and met her gaze. 'There's more I haven't told you, but I need you to trust me when I say it's nothing to do with us. It's connected to this job and isn't my place to tell.'

'Jack Watson, you're impossible. I told you earlier you were hopeless. This poor girl doesn't need half a story.'

Hannah bustled in and set a tray down on the table. She passed steaming mugs of tea to them both, and before Jack could say another word she took over. Gemma tried not to smile at his obvious bemusement. She struggled to follow the convoluted explanation that involved Jack's boss; Hannah's sister, who appeared to be a big Hollywood star; and a scheme to pull off a big wedding surprise.

'Goodness me.' Gemma didn't know what else to say for a minute and picked up her mug, blowing on the surface of her tea to cool it down before taking a sip. 'I hate to ask, and I do trust Jack.' Gemma hesitated. 'It's probably not my business, but . . .'

'You're wondering why was I upset

earlier?' Hannah finished for her.

'You weren't talking about me, were you?'

'No.' Hannah gave a deep sigh and rubbed at her forehead. 'I'd just received a text from my fiancé.' She stroked her bare ring finger and sucked in a deep breath. 'I suppose I should say ex-fiancé, but I'm not used to the idea yet. He told me it wasn't fair to keep lying to me. He's been seeing someone else and is going to, um, marry her at Christmas.'

'What a coward. Do you know the other woman?'

'Oh, yes. She used to be my best friend,' Hannah scoffed.

Trying to imagine April doing such a thing was impossible and Gemma struggled to know to respond.

'Poor Jack here got the brunt of it, I'm afraid.' Hannah managed a slight laugh. 'I blubbered all over him and he was very kind to put up with me.'

Gemma felt a complete fool. 'He's the kindest man I know,' she murmured and glanced over at him, the cool green of his unrevealing eyes worrying her. 'I hope he's big enough to forgive a stupid woman.'

'It's time I went,' Hannah said. 'I'll leave you two to sort things out.' Her firm stare never wavered. 'Don't forget how fragile love can be. Treasure it. Pride is all very well, but in the end it won't make you happy. I've made mistakes with Greg but was too stubborn to admit it, and I'm sure that's partly the reason he left.' She leaned in close enough to whisper in Gemma's ear. 'Good luck.'

Left on their own, an uneasy silence filled the room, and Gemma wondered who would be the first to break it. She was so afraid of saying the wrong thing that she literally couldn't speak.

'You're not stupid.' Jack's serious tone of voice made her shiver. 'Maybe not very smart at times.' The beginnings of a smile pulled at the edges of his mouth. 'But definitely not stupid.' A full-blown grin spread across his face and the knot of tension in the pit of her stomach unravelled.

'Are we okay?' she dared to ask, and he replied with a gentle kiss on her forehead.

'Of course we are.' His eyes darkened. 'My vanity appreciates it that you were jealous — but don't ever do that to me again.' He brushed a lock of hair from her face. 'You scared me half to death. When I opened the car door, you were so still and pale.' His voice cracked and he struggled not to completely break down. 'If anything had happened to you I'd never have forgiven myself.'

'I'm more sorry than I can say.' Gemma made an effort to smile. 'If I hadn't been so keen to see you, all this wouldn't have happened.'

Jack's usual swagger returned and he flashed one of his killer smiles. She hadn't been able to resist them at seventeen and they still made her weak at the knees. 'Yeah, well, I have that effect on women.'

Playfully she smacked his hand. 'From now on there's only one woman you're going to have under your spell.'

'Oh yeah? And who might that be?' he teased, pulling her into his arms. Suddenly he pulled away. 'Heck, Gemma, I forgot I was going to take you to the hospital.'

She had, too, with all the chaos that'd gone on. 'All I need is a little more spoiling,' she told him.

'Are you sure?'

'Absolutely.' His eyebrows rose but he didn't attempt to argue. 'Now I'm here, why don't you show me around the house?' She drew a hand dramatically across her throat. 'I swear I won't tell anyone what I've seen and promise not to write an article for the local newspaper on the Cornish Honeymoon House.'

Jack stood and held out his hand, gently pulling her up to join him. 'Your wish is my command.'

* * *

244

The next hour was wonderful as they explored every nook and cranny of the beautiful house. Gemma decided that the best part of the whole thing for her was Jack's enthusiasm for the project. He was excited about everything, from finding the perfect set of outside gates — thanks to Hannah — to other smaller achievements. His favourite story was about one of the carpenters who discovered a glass bottle under the floorboards of the old nursery with letters written in the late 1800s by one of the young Dean children.

'Hannah had a great time talking to old Mrs. Green,' he said. 'She worked there as a young girl and told him all kinds of stories about the family and the entertaining that used to go on, up to the beginning of the Second World War.'

Gemma smiled. 'I love it when history becomes real.' She suddenly had a thought and wondered if he'd think her crazy.

'Come on out with it.' He'd always

been a good mind-reader where she was concerned.

'Thea is fascinated by old houses, right?' she asked, and he nodded in agreement. 'I'm sure she'd love to have a written history of West Dean House when she moves in.'

'Genius. And I know the perfect person to put something together.' His stare deepened as he fixed his gleaming eyes on her.

'Me?'

'Of course. You're local, so you're familiar with the place. You can pick Hannah's brains and interrogate Mrs. Green some more.'

'But I'm not a writer.'

'Stop making excuses. For now I'm talking about something informal.' His voice sped up. 'I'm thinking more a collection of short pieces. Maybe put it in a pretty journal sort of thing.'

She hugged him tight. 'I may be mad to say yes, but I'd love to give it a try.'

'You'll be paid.' She tried to protest but he dismissed it outright. 'Don't argue. Everyone else is being well rewarded for their work and you'll be no different. Paul wouldn't have it any other way.'

This decisive side of Jack intrigued her. As a younger man it'd been there under the surface, but he'd grown into it now in the same way he'd matured into his striking good looks.

'What will you do when this job is finished?' The question was blurted out before Gemma could stop to think. She hurried to explain herself, stammering out her words. She'd observed his love for this sort of work and couldn't imagine him going back to the more pedestrian kind of business deals he usually performed.

'Don't fret,' he reassured her. 'I know what you're getting at. The answer is, I'm not sure. Paul knows I'm unsettled and we'll talk it over when I'm done here.' He gave her a sheepish grin and told her the story about Hannah catching him singing. 'I don't intend to take it back up seriously, but I might like to join a choir or amateur operatic group. I realised a long time ago that although I was a decent singer, so are plenty of other people. It takes a lot more to make a living from it.' He played with one of Gemma's curls and smiled. 'We've a lot to sort out you and me, but we'll get there.'

A surge of love for this special man soared through Gemma, lifting her spirits. 'I know we will.'

'Time to get you home, I think.'

'What about my car?'

'I'll get it towed to the garage in the morning,' Jack declared, and she didn't protest. 'I don't know about you, but I'm starving. Is it okay if we eat at the Green Dragon?'

He could've suggested bread and cheese and Gemma wouldn't have minded. She couldn't regret coming to see him, despite all the turmoil that'd resulted. Sometimes a person had to follow their heart. She hadn't done that enough in her life, but from today she intended to change.

21

There was nothing of the good-humoured charmer about Jack today. The grim-faced man clutching the steering wheel and glaring at the road could've been a stranger. He'd barely said a word since picking Gemma up, and when she suggested he tell her more about his parents, his answer was blunt and to the point.

'You'll see when you get there. I'd rather you made up your own mind.'

They crossed the Tamar bridge into Devon, and Gemma struggled to remember the last time she'd been to Plymouth shopping. When did she ever have a day off with nothing to do?

'We'll be at the house in about five minutes,' Jack said, and she almost teased him about not being on their way to an execution. One glance at his stony features changed her mind, however, and instead she lowered the mirror and fiddled with her hair.

He turned right at the next corner before slowing down, and about half-way along the road he pulled into a narrow driveway. 'This is it.' He nodded towards the large detached house and Gemma checked it out, noticing the well-manicured garden and immaculate black paint.

She closed her hand over his. 'We'll be all right. No matter what.'

'Yeah. I know.' Jack tried to smile. 'Let's get this over with.' He got out of the car, and when Gemma joined him he grabbed her hand as if she was a life preserver thrown to a drowning man.

'Your mum is looking forward to seeing you,' she gently reminded him.

'I know.' Jack's heavy sigh pulled at her heart. 'Thanks. You're too good for me.'

'As long as you realise it,' Gemma teased.

'Oh, I do.' He tightened his hand around hers again. 'Come on.'

Before they even reached the door, it opened and a stern-featured man waited on the step for them to join him. Jack had plainly got his tall, rangy build from his father, but not Philip Watson's sandy hair, pale blue eyes and ruddy English complexion. They struggled their way through stilted introductions and Gemma was scrutinised with no hint of apology.

'In you go. She's waiting,' Jack's father announced and stood back to let them enter the square hall. 'The kettle's boiling. I'll make the tea.' He disappeared into the kitchen and left them staring at each other.

'A man of few words,' Gemma observed, pleased when Jack cracked a smile. 'Take me to your mum.' He nodded and headed for the half-open door facing them. Gemma sensed his hesitation and caught the hitch in his breath before he kept going.

'Here we are.' His bright greeting sounded false to Gemma's ears and she mentally crossed her fingers as she followed him into the room.

The first thing to hit her was the oppressive heat, and the next was the sight of Jack's mother struggling to her feet to greet them. Traces of Mediterranean beauty remained in Maria Watson's dark eyes and full red lips, but her olive skin was tinged with the sheen of ill-health. Her grey-streaked dark hair was scraped into a loose bun.

'You must be Gemma.' Maria's frail voice still held a trace of her Italian accent. 'Jack told me about you last time he came. I know you're very special to him.'

Gemma's throat tightened. She had no idea he'd spoken to his mother about her, and certainly not in such an intimate way. 'He is to me too,' she said. Maria's spontaneous smile left Gemma with no doubt that this was where Jack's own bewitching smile came from. She blurted out her observation and Maria's broad smile took years off her strained features.

'Would you care to see some photos of Jack when he was little?'

'I'd love to.' Gemma caught Jack rolling his eyes and poked his arm. 'It's what we women like to do. Go and help your dad with the tea.' An uncomfortable silence filled the room and she guessed she'd said something out of place.

'That's a wonderful idea,' Maria agreed with a new hint of firmness to her voice. 'Don't hurry back. He wants to talk to you.'

'Since when?' Jack retorted.

'Since my doctor told him he must make an effort if he wants to help me get better.'

Under the power of his mother's pleading gaze and the waves of sympathy coming from Gemma, what choice did he have? But if they thought nearly forty years of harsh indifference could be wiped out in one afternoon, they were sadly deluded.

'Listen to him, Jack, please,' Maria pleaded. 'He won't tell you about his own father because he considers it a modern weakness to blame everything that goes wrong on someone's upbringing. His father was an appalling man. If you think Philip was hard on you, he was nothing in comparison with Bert Watson.' She shuddered as she spoke his name. 'In his own way your father always wanted the best for you, but he simply didn't know how to show it.'

Jack bit the inside of his cheek. 'I'll listen, and I'll try for your sake. But I'm making no promises.'

'Thank you.'

His own mother shouldn't have to thank him for agreeing to be a mature man instead of an impetuous boy. A lump formed in his throat, and it was only the soft touch of Gemma's fingers on his arm that kept him somewhat together. He nodded and trailed off towards the kitchen, feeling two pairs of eyes on his back all the way.

'Sent you in for our little chat, did she?' The touch of amusement in Philip's voice surprised him. 'Maria couldn't be subtle if she tried. It's the Italian way.' He shrugged and gestured to Jack to sit down. 'We might as well be comfortable. She won't let us back in until we've shared our innermost thoughts and hugged and cried like that idiotic doctor wants.'

'Heck, is that really what you've got in mind?' Jack couldn't hide his horror. 'I thought we'd exchange a few grievances and shake hands like regular Englishmen then never talk about it again.'

'Do you really think that'll be enough to make you hate me less?' Philip murmured, his voice rough with emotion.

'I don't . . . '

'Yes, you do. Admit it.'

The stern army officer persona returned and Jack remonstrated with himself, determined not to slip back into his usual way of dealing with his father's brusque manner. He took a couple of deep, calming breaths and looked Philip straight in the eye. 'I did for a long time. Now that I'm at a better place in my life and have Gemma back with me, I can feel sorry for you.'

'I don't want your sympathy,' Philip snapped.

'Tough.' Jack's retort startled his father, who went oddly quiet. 'You treated me like one of your recruits. Nothing I did was good enough for you.' He hesitated, choosing his words carefully. 'Mum says you learned your ways from your father, and if that's the case I do feel sorry for you; but I don't intend to be the same. If I have children I hope I'll show my love by encouraging them instead of putting them down.'

Philip leaned forward and rested his elbows on the table, clutching his bent head in his hands. 'I didn't know how else to be,' he rasped.

Jack impulsively rested a hand on his father's shoulder, unable to remember the last time they'd touched apart from formally shaking hands. He knew Philip would hate breaking down in front of him so tried to think of something to ease his guilt. 'You were right about one thing, though,' he said.

'What was that?' His father sounded puzzled.

'The idea I was good enough to pursue singing as a career was typical teenaged cockiness on my part.'

Philip shrugged. 'Maybe, but I should've let you find out that yourself. You wouldn't have resented me as much then.'

In a nutshell he'd encapsulated Jack's main gripe with his father: the fact he'd never been allowed to make his own mistakes, and when he'd made them despite Philip's rigid control he'd been punished. Haltingly he tried to explain, and watched his father struggle to understand. The knowledge that Philip was trying meant everything.

'I don't expect you to forgive me,' Philip hurried on, stopping Jack's attempt to interrupt. 'Do you think for your mother's sake you can visit us more? Maybe we can paper over the cracks enough to — '

'Fool her? Aren't we better than that?' Jack challenged, and a flash of what appeared to be admiration coloured his father's eyes. 'I think we could be.'

'When did you get to be so clever?' The touch of irony was far more the man Jack knew. Philip loudly cleared his throat. 'Gemma appears to be a decent young woman.'

Jack could think of far better ways to describe the woman he loved, but in his father's book that was high praise.

'She's the same girl you, um, were friends with that summer in Cornwall, isn't she? The one who sent all those . . . ' His voice trailed away and an unpleasant suspicion formed in Jack's mind.

'All those what?'

'Letters.' The curt reply sliced through Jack and he fought back the urge to say something he'd regret later. 'They arrived every day for months. I told your mother to tear them up and throw them away.'

'Why?' Jack whispered. 'I thought Gemma didn't care about me anymore.'

'You were on the brink of taking important exams that would determine your future. You didn't need to be distracted by a pretty face.' Philip frowned. 'Your mother didn't approve, but she agreed to do what I asked.'

As usual. Jack didn't want to be bitter about his mother but it was hard. He forced himself to remember what was important. 'Gemma and I love each other — we always have done — and that's all that matters now.'

'I haven't been as kind to your mother as I should have. Don't make the same mistakes as me. That's all I'll say, Jack.' Philip pushed the chair back and stood up. 'I think we'd better take the tea in or they might think we've killed each other.'

For several seconds they looked at each other without speaking. Jack briefly considered hugging his father, but the warning in Philip's eyes told him to leave well alone. He nodded and left him to it. Pushing the kitchen door open, he saw his mother and Gemma sitting together on the sofa, laughing happily and surrounded by photograph albums. On the coffee table there was a small wooden box he didn't recognise, and as he walked closer he saw a bunch of letters sticking out of the top. His stomach roiled as he caught sight of Gemma's distinctive handwriting.

He leaned down and picked one up and fingered it cautiously as though it might explode. Both women looked at him with concern in their eyes. 'Dad told me you'd torn them up,' he said to his mother.

Philip came in carrying a large tray. 'No. I said I told her to tear them up. There's a difference.' A rare twinkle of humour tugged at his mouth and for a minute Jack almost wondered if his father might laugh for once. The way today was going, he wouldn't be surprised.

'Your mum said I could take them

home with us,' Gemma said softly. 'We'll read them later.'

'Tea everyone?' Philip asked, and Jack somehow managed to agree and offer to help. A few minutes later he sneaked a look around at everyone and smiled. If any outsider saw them sitting around drinking tea and eating cake, they'd think they were a regular family who did this every Sunday afternoon.

When Jack and Gemma left there were plenty of hugs and kisses, although he and his father stuck to their usual handshake, which was done with a new warmth. Jack doubted they'd ever have the sort of close relationship he saw with other fathers and sons, but he was content.

All the way back to Trewarne, Gemma rested her head on Jack's shoulder, and they talked idly about everything and nothing. 'Do you want to have supper first?' she asked when they arrived at her house, but Jack shook his head. Quietly they sat on the same sofa where they'd sneaked a few stolen kisses in front of the television all those years ago, and read the outpourings of Gemma's teenage heart. The first letters were full of exciting plans for their future, but later her anxiety started to seep through, turning to heartbreak when she had heard nothing back from him. The last one was written on Christmas Day. Gemma told him goodbye and said she'd never forget him. Finally she wished him well for the rest of his life.

Jack brushed at some dampness on his cheek and realised it was tears. 'All that matters now is that you know I never stopped loving you,' he said.

Gemma wrapped her hands around his face and kissed him. Her fragrant scent surrounded him and he knew he was one lucky man. Not everyone got a second chance at love.

22

Epilogue — New Year's Day

'I'd say you've done a pretty good job, Mr. Watson,' Gemma declared as she stood with Jack at the rear of the ballroom and gazed out over the crowd of assembled guests.

'Only because of the incredible support of the soon-to-be Mrs. Watson.' Jack beamed and lifted her hand to his lips. He brushed a soft kiss over her fingers and lingered on the glittering diamond he'd sneaked into her Christmas stocking. 'It turned out pretty well, I'd say.'

'Hannah did a wonderful job.'

'She did indeed.' He gave her a conspiratorial wink. Luckily the secret had stayed that way. Gemma usually hated deceit of any sort, but she'd happily made an exception in that case and was lucky enough to be with Jack when the newly married couple arrived. Thea's face when she 'discovered' that West Dean House wasn't a hotel but a wedding present from her adoring husband had been a piece of Oscar-worthy acting.

'Is Hannah here tonight?' Gemma asked.

'Nope. She's on a ski trip in France with a bunch of her girlfriends. I have a feeling the après-ski activities attracted them all far more than the slopes.'

'I'm glad she's not moping.'

'She's not the sort of woman to stay down for long.' Jack slid his arm around Gemma's waist and pulled her closer. 'Did you have time to pack this afternoon?'

'I did indeed. I can't wait to see Nashville. You've told me so much, I feel I know the place already.' They were leaving in the morning for an extended visit while they made their own plans for the future. Thankfully Gemma didn't have to worry about the shop because April had declared her interest in buying it with money she'd been secretly saving for years. She planned to use her love of knitting to open a wool shop, even though the idea upset her mother — something April didn't seem bothered about anymore. She and Harry were slowly exploring their new relationship, and it made Gemma happier than she could say to see them together.

'Everyone's going to want to hear you talk, but they won't understand half of what you're saying and vice versa,' Jack warned. 'It'll be a huge change from here.'

'That's exactly what I want — a huge change. I've been stuck in a rut for far too long. You've shaken me out of it and I've no intention of going back in.'

'Good. We'll find our own road and enjoy the journey together.' Jack's infectious smile warmed Gemma all the way to her toes. He gestured towards the band. 'Come on. They're playing our song.'

The sound of Mariah Carey's 'Endless Love' startled Gemma. In that long-ago summer of 1994 it'd been their favourite song, summing up everything they felt about each other. Tears welled in her eyes. 'Did you request it?'

'Of course.' He touched her chin and tilted her to him for a magical kiss. 'I never forgot, either. Happy New Year.'